Break A Leg
Copyright 2025
Independently published by Briar Townsend
All rights reserved

No portion of this work may be reproduced in whole or in part without the express permission of the author. If referenced in another work, credit must be given. This work may not be used to train or inform artificial intelligence or related technologies. All rights remain with the estate of the author upon their death unless and until the copyright expires.

Break A Leg is a work of fiction. Any references, resemblances to, or mentions of real people, places, or things are either coincidental or fictionalised, and not intended as a realistic depiction or representation of said entity.

Cover art & design: Milo Leonardini (Instagram @chalkydel)

Print ISBN: 979-8-9923066-0-6

Break A Leg
a queer novella

by
Briar Townsend

Content Guidance

This story contains allusions to and mentions of transphobia and homophobia.

Part of the story takes place in a medical establishment, though no specific procedures occur on the page.

While generally a "fluffy" story, it's possible these topics may cause you distress. Please take the space you need before, during, and/or after reading to look after yourself.

Table of Contents

Part One	1
Part Two	7
Part Three	63

PART ONE

Lucas is currently experiencing one of his best Sunday afternoons in recent memory. This morning started with a positive email from his publisher, he spent an hour on the phone with his sisters (all back home in Barnsley fawning over Cat's new baby), then it was a picnic lunch with his best mate Nathan and Nathan's partner Zakir.

At the moment, he's enjoying the unseasonably mild summer by walking his two dogs around the neighbourhood for much longer than the weather normally allows. Neither Lucas nor his dogs tolerate the heat very well.

Moving to Brighton in his late twenties was one of the best decisions Lucas ever made. He saved as much as he could from each of his book releases until he was able to afford a small house (attached, but a *house* that he owns), then moved himself all the way down the country to the coast with just his laptop and a few boxes of clothes.

He's built a life for himself in his almost three years here: Lucas has his hidden cafes where he writes, local restaurants where he goes on dates (when he finds someone to ask), trains that he takes into London when he needs to meet with his editor, parks where he picnics with mates and walks his beloved dogs. He has his routines and lifestyle figured out, even if the initial change from a smaller, Northern town to this touristy beach city has been a significant adjustment. Lucas is doing well for himself, established in his career as a narrative nonfiction writer, and settled into his life.

There's only one thing missing, a longing that comes to him late at night or first thing in the morning. Lucas is looking for someone to share his charmed life with. It's not that he's lonely, really, but he's a serial monogamist and he has a hard time finding people to date between his odd schedule as a writer and his personal peculiarities. Nevermind that he's never been won over by anything less than a brilliant mind ruled by a generous heart. And whoever he dates has to love his dogs at least as well as him.

Nathan says his standards are too high, but Lucas reminds him that not everyone bumps into their soulmate (who happens to be an actual combination print model and indie singer) the first week of uni.

Lucas has had relationships, but none that lasted longer than a few months. He hoped that when he moved here, to Brighton, the gayest place in England according to most, that he'd have more luck. But he's not very comfortable in the club scene, preferring a chat over tea or a night at the theatre, and so here he is: single, 31 years old, and following his perfect dogs around the pavement while soaking in the end of summer, privately wishing he had a partner by his side.

But then Lucas rounds the corner to his street and the sun shines a ray brighter, focusing on his most recent romantic interest: his new(ish) neighbour who's been renting the house next door for the past few months. They've never met officially despite sharing a wall, a garden, and a propensity for odd hours.

Lucas doesn't even know their name yet, but he's observed that they love his dogs, they're incredibly fit, and they avoid neighbours like a plague despite having regular visitors. And right now, as Lucas and the dogs approach the building, the sun hits their upturned face and Lucas hears the angels' chorus.

"Alright?" Lucas greets, his dogs now pulling him along as fast as their broad shoulders can carry them. Adopting two young staffies from the local shelter hadn't been in his immediate plans when he moved here, but Nathan brought him along while choosing a dog as a birthday surprise for Zakir, and Lucas had been absolutely gone for these two wriggling bundles of joy since the first bark.

"Oh, erm, hello." The mystery neighbour doesn't look at Lucas, instead holding out their hands to the dogs as they kneel to give them attention. Lucas appreciates their focus since he firmly believes that everyone should immediately fawn over his perfect animals if they have any sense at all. "I like their new outfits."

Lucas is surprised at the attempt at conversation, but then again, his dogs do have that effect on most people. "They get new bandanas at the groomers each month, *if* they behave, and they went just yesterday."

Mystery neighbour is even more interesting up close, a camera bag over their shoulder and a claw clip holding back their short, curly brown hair. They're innately gentle despite being a few inches taller and broader than Lucas, cooing at his dogs with a soft expression in their eyes.

"What sort of dogs are they?" They ask while Annie puts both front paws on their shoulders and starts to sniffle at their face. They don't seem to mind, continuing to love on both dogs with a shy smile. And Lucas is falling hard for their gorgeous, deep voice, like something from a noir film. He's never heard them speak a full sentence before today.

"Staffordshire bull terriers, what some would call the 'nannie dog' because they're good with kids. Purebred, even though I found them at the shelter. Too small or something, so they were abandoned there, but I think they're perfect." Lucas watches how the dogs act with his neighbour/crush, no hesitancy in climbing all over them.

He's caught the three of them out in the garden together most mornings, running and playing while Lucas makes his coffee and watches through the kitchen window. He's never interrupted, glad that the girls bring joy to another person, especially if that person is remarkably shy.

"How could anyone leave you, hm?" They have Hallie's face cradled in their palms, asking her as if expecting a response. She wags and wags and licks their cheek, Annie getting jealous and trying to shove her out of the way, making them laugh. There's a nose scrunch and a hint of a dimple and Lucas may need to propose.

"Oi, girls, behave yourselves." Lucas tugs on their leads, both of them turning to look at him with wide, innocent eyes. It's a good thing he committed hard to their training early on because those puppy eyes could tame a bear, even with his years of hard won immunity to their cuteness. "Sorry about that."

"S'alright. They're sweet." Brushing their palms along their high waisted trousers, they stand up and put a hand on each of the girl's broad foreheads in a sort of goodbye pat. Glancing briefly up at Lucas (who experiences a flutter of electricity in his chest when he sees clear, sage green eyes), they add, "Well, I was just..."

They point behind themselves in the vague direction of the city centre before letting their hand drop again.

"Lucas." Lucas blurts out as they turn away, not wanting to go another day without exchanging names. Maybe if he's lucky they'll work up to talk of the weather by Christmas.

They turn back to him with a furrowed brow, as if surprised, so he continues the thought. "I'm Lucas. Just couldn't remember if I'd introduced myself and was starting to feel a bit rude. Haven't even offered you to come round for a cuppa yet, but my name is a start."

"Lucas..." They repeat, scanning him up and down for a moment before flashing another shy smile that's hidden away almost immediately. "I'm Matty...I'll get back to you about tea."

And then Matty giggles at Lucas before hurrying away in earnest, one hand holding tight to their camera bag and the other playing nervously with the curls at the back of their head. Lucas watches them go, heart beating so fast it may take flight. If he's not mistaken, that was mild flirting.

"Girls, mark my words." Lucas squats down to the dogs' level, conspiring in a faux hushed whisper after Matty is around the corner. "Matty is going to change our lives."

6

PART TWO

Lucas doesn't see Matty again for almost three weeks, at least not officially. He sees Matty in the garden with the dogs, listens to them singing along to ABBA through the thin wall of the entryway, sees them hurrying away a few times when he's coming or going with the dogs.

But they don't stop for a chat again. No more giggles, no acknowledgement of Lucas's existence except for a moment he overheard during one of their morning visits with the dogs, asking if their dad was taking good care of them and giving them enough treats. Lucas almost melted onto the kitchen floor, but then the moment passed and the dogs were scrabbling at the back door to be let in for their breakfast.

The problem is that Lucas is enchanted. He catches glimpses and builds the rest of the picture, sees Matty in all black hurrying into an uber and wonders if it's work, hears what he assumes are family members out in the garden one weekend because the voices are fond and familiar with Matty, notices a new potted plant in front of Matty's door and imagines them tending to it with a watering can and a smile. If only they weren't so shy, but Lucas isn't going to push. If Matty wants privacy, Lucas can certainly respect that.

But they did say they'd get back to Lucas about tea...

It's not until Saturday night a few weeks later, near the end of September, that he has any actual contact with Matty again. Lucas is chopping vegetables for a hearty soup while the dogs circle his space when he hears an incredible crash coming from next door. In an instant, Lucas decides to break that commitment to leave Matty to themself.

That crash was way too loud to be Matty just dropping something, more likely a large piece of furniture, or god fucking forbid Matty themself falling. Lucas sets down his knife and scrabbles towards the front door with the dogs close behind, not hesitating for a second while emergency scenarios flash through his mind. He throws on a denim jacket and tells the dogs to stay even as they whine, running down his own front steps and right back up Matty's in ten seconds flat.

"Matty!" Lucas knocks solidly on the door three times and waits, shivering in the constant breeze. It gets so chilly at night once summer passes. He doesn't hear anything from inside so he knocks twice more and adds, "Matty, it's Lucas. Is everything alright?"

Why don't these houses have doorbells? It's a harkening back to their original construction, he's sure. But right now he doesn't give a damn about historical charm. At least with a doorbell he'd be sure Matty's heard him.

After a delay, there's some sort of shouted reply and Lucas breathes properly for the first time in over a minute. He couldn't make out the words but at least Matty's conscious. He waits a full thirty seconds, counting in his head before knocking again. And just as he's about to do so the door creaks open and Matty appears. "Fuck, you look - "

"Hi, Lucas." Matty is flushed, seemingly embarrassed, but Lucas is far too distracted to notice because Matty looks *gorgeous*. Their hair is curled into soft ringlets, they've got a full face of makeup on, and they're wearing a mid-thigh bodycon dress that looks straight off a runway. "How are you?"

Lucas shakes his head to refocus and shoves his hands into his pockets, remembering why he rushed over here in the first place. "Me? How are you?! I heard - well I don't know what I heard, but it was loud and not in a fun way."

"The fun way...*Oh*." Matty flushes deeper, eyes widening in understanding at the insinuation. "No, I wasn't...I'm alone, I just sort of tripped a bit, but I'm fine."

"You're sure? I can send the girls over to play doctor if you've twisted anything." Lucas laughs at his own joke, relieved to see Matty give him another shy smile. They shift their weight and wince before clearing their face back to neutral and looking down at their doormat.

"I'm sure they're excellent nurses, but I'm alright, really." Matty tucks a piece of hair behind their ear and Lucas notices a dainty, dangling pearl earring to match the necklace across their collarbones. So beautiful, but Lucas is resolutely not going to point that out and make Matty uncomfortable.

"As long as you're sure." Lucas offers Matty a genuine smile because despite his worry he does sort of like this person already. He gestures at his own front door to add, "I'm staying in tonight if you need anything."

"I know where to find you." Matty confirms, returning Lucas's grin before glancing away again, both hands holding onto the door as their face falls. If Lucas didn't know any better he'd think Matty was holding themself up...

"Right, well, bye then." Lucas retreats down the steps, turning back to glance at Matty once more just as the door closes.

Back inside his own home, Lucas greets his worried dogs with his usual nonsensical babble, telling them that Matty is alright and aren't they just the best dogs in the world for being so worried about their friend. He goes back to his kitchen, finishes chopping, and sets his soup to simmer before opening up his laptop. He may as well get some writing in tonight.

***

An hour and a half later, Lucas is typing furiously, glasses reflecting his laptop, the remains of his dinner off to the side while his mind composes and revises in real time...and then there's a knock at his front door. The dogs immediately sprint over, woken from their sofa nap by the visitor, and ready to beg for attention.

"It's alright girls, I'll get it." Lucas sighs, hoping he doesn't lose his train of thought. He was in the middle of an excellent paragraph about autumn leaves and he'd just found the metaphorical resonance he'd been searching for. "Back to the sofa, go on."

Hallie and Annie look up at him, their whole bodies wagging with anticipation of a visitor, until he points over at the sofa and they trot back across the room, falling on top of themselves. It's a good thing they're so obedient because there's two of them and only one Lucas. They have a habit of forgetting the concept of personal space whenever a new person enters the home. He's working on it.

But when Lucas opens the front door he's the most confused he's been in a long while. "Matty?"

"You're wearing glasses." Is what Matty chooses to say instead of any sort of explanation. Lucas isn't sure what to do about that seeing as there's at least three metaphorical elephants clogging the doorway.

"I am, yes. Was just getting some writing done." Lucas glances over at the dogs for a moment, as if they could clue him in to what's happening. They just stare back, not a thought in their heads, waiting for his permission to say hello to Matty, too.

"Oh...should I go?" Matty worries at their bottom lip, still dressed in the same ensemble as earlier except...

"Is there a reason you're on the ground?" Lucas has to ask. It's not everyday that his gorgeous neighbour knocks on his door only to sit on the stoop and stare up at him like some sort of land mermaid. Those gorgeous, kind eyes are increasingly distracting.

"I crawled to get here and didn't see anything to pull myself up." Matty answers simply, as if that much was obvious.

"And you crawled to my house because...?" Lucas tilts his head, removing his glasses and setting them on the hall table that holds his keys and wallet. This is turning out to be a very strange evening.

"Oh, I've broken my ankle. Quite badly, as it turns out." Matty glances down at their legs which are just out of Lucas's field of vision. "I walked on it for a few minutes, but that proved impossible soon enough. Slithering seemed a step too far. Or I suppose a slither too far."

"You've broken your ankle." Lucas confirms, one hand still holding his front door open, the other already reaching for his car keys. Matty is the most interesting person alive and right now all Lucas can think about is how to get them to a doctor. Land mermaids can't be going around with broken ankles.

"I have, yes. The left one." Matty sighs, shifting their legs around to show the visual evidence and Lucas almost wishes they hadn't because that ankle could turn an army medic's stomach. "And in my new shoes, too."

"That was the crash I heard earlier?" Lucas should've known, should've recognised that Matty was clearly in pain when they answered their own door earlier in the night. They were essentially holding themself up.

"Unfortunately, yes. Sorry about that." Matty's hair is pulled away from their face with a clip, but that doesn't stop them from nervously running their fingers through it. "I try to keep the noise to a courteous level, as the walls are thin in some rooms."

"I'm taking you to A&E." Lucas moves the door until it's fully open so Matty can watch as he grabs his phone and coat to go along with his keys and wallet. He kicks off his slippers and hastily ties a pair of black Vans to replace them, all while Matty observes him with a conflicted look.

"Are you sure? I wouldn't have bothered you, only I can't drive like this and even if I could I don't have a car anymore. Sold it when I moved." Matty pulls themself along until they're just inside Lucas's threshold, brightening a bit when they see the dogs waiting for them. "Could I say hello to the dogs before we go?"

"Of course." Lucas has to smile. Here Matty is, in the middle of a medical emergency (yet miraculously calm), and still they want to cuddle with his animals. Despite the circumstances, Lucas's crush blossoms. "Hallie, Annie, come here."

They tumble over each other in their haste, Annie reaching Matty first and licking them right across the nose, making them splutter as they laugh. Lucas allows them a few moments of fun before he calls the dogs back again so they can get going, because the dogs can't tag along for this outing. "Could I help you to the car?"

"You don't have to. I could, um, maybe I could try crawling again." Matty sounds sincere and Lucas isn't sure if he should laugh or not. He doesn't know Matty well enough to know if that was excellently delivered sarcasm or a genuine suggestion.

"I'd rather you didn't." Lucas squats down and slides an arm around Matty's waist, pulling their body up to standing again. They're taller than Lucas, which he knew, but it's more apparent when he's being used like a crutch.

Matty smells like violets and rosewater, subtle but sweet. Lucas makes a concerted effort not to hide his nose against Matty's neck and build a home there.

"Say goodbye, girls." Lucas calls to the dogs before closing the door.

"Goodbye." Matty gives the dogs a small wave, and Lucas hears them whining as he locks up behind them. His dogs are a smidge codependent, preferring never to be left home alone, but needs must.

"You don't have any shoes on." Lucas observes, still standing on his doorstep with Matty leaning against his side.

"Couldn't get any heels to fit over the left foot now it's all swollen and nothing else went with the outfit." Matty shrugs, and Lucas shouldn't want to kiss them so badly right now. But this is the most they've ever interacted and Lucas wishes they could share tea in his kitchen while Matty keeps talking for the rest of eternity. Their words are slow and measured, like honey drizzled on the air.

"I should have some slides in my gym bag, if you'd like to borrow those for the night." Lucas suggests as he helps Matty walk towards the car. It's very slow going since Matty is essentially hopping on one leg and Lucas is learning that their tall, gangly Bambi legs are prone to tumbles.

"I'm gonna kill Zakir." Matty mumbles, wincing as their left foot accidentally brushes the ground. "Break a leg, he says."

"Zakir?" Lucas asks, wondering if there's any universe where it's the same Zakir that he's become good mates with through Nathan. But of course that's astronomically unlikely.

"Friend from work. Well...started as a friend from work. Now we're sort of codependent badgers." Matty groans when they see how much further the walk to the car is while Lucas wonders how metaphorical the badger image is meant to be. "Sorry, shouldn't be complaining. I've ruined your evening and I'm complaining."

"You haven't ruined anything, Matty. I was just getting some writing done." Lucas pauses to readjust his hold on Matty, moving his hand lower to their waist rather than their side and pulling their arm across his shoulders, something he should've done before they started moving. His mum was a nurse for god's sake. He should know the basics of first aid.

"You write?" Matty sounds genuinely curious, hopping easier with Lucas's new arm positioning. Only another short stretch to the car now and much more manageable this way.

"Let's get you in the car and then we can talk more." Lucas has never been more glad to have recently cleaned his car. He loves his dogs, but they shed more than should be physically possible.

"You don't mind?" Matty asks, and they sound surprised, as if expecting Lucas to tell them to shut up.

"Talking to you?" Lucas turns his head briefly and sees them flushed. They were a bit pale from the pain earlier, so maybe they're just feeling the effort of this nontraditional walk to his vehicle. "No, Matty, I don't mind. You've a lovely voice."

"Oh...thank you." Matty definitely flushes further at the compliment. Lucas tucks that information away for later.

He certainly doesn't love that Matty's in pain, but it's nice to finally get to know them as more than...Lucas is starting to see the wisdom of the badger metaphor, picturing all the times that Matty has disappeared into the night, scurrying away without a word.

"Back seat, don't you think?" Lucas tilts his head toward the car, assuming that Matty will want to elevate their clearly destroyed ankle on the drive. It's not far but it's far enough.

"Alright." Matty's back to being shy, and Lucas, true to his promise, isn't going to push it. He helps Matty get situated and offers a pillow for underneath their foot as extra cushion.

"Is this a dog pillow?" Matty asks, examining the printed fabric in the dim light of the streetlamp before tucking it beneath their swollen ankle and wincing in pain.

"Oi, it's a better pillow than I have on my own bed, I'll have you know." Lucas teases. And he's not lying. His dogs have the best of everything.

"I wasn't complaining, only asking." Matty buckles themself in and waits for Lucas to close the door before getting into the seat directly in front of them.

Lucas pulls the car away from the house as they get underway in awkward silence. He doesn't really know Matty besides the small moments he's seen and the fact that they're currently in his back seat with a broken bone. It's only now that it occurs to Lucas that Matty didn't call anyone else to bring them to hospital, or maybe they did and no one was available. But this is a huge show of trust from Matty and Lucas will take it for what it is.

"Lucas?" Matty asks after almost ten minutes of quiet. They sound hesitant, like they aren't sure if they're allowed to ask questions.

"You alright? We should be there soon." Lucas glances in the rearview mirror as he pulls up to a traffic light. The streetlamps cast Matty in an artificial glow, and he can't read how they're feeling. He certainly hopes they've at least taken an anti-inflammatory dose by now, but he didn't think to ask before they left.

"What do you write?" Matty asks, looking wistfully off through the window, staring towards nothing at all.

Lucas wishes he knew what they were thinking about and how Matty even remembers what Lucas does for work in the midst of what must be excruciating pain. "I'm a nonfiction writer. Narrative nonfiction. Not sure if that's your thing, but my most popular book is called *Can't Get Through The Glass*. It's about queer people living in small towns and how - "

"You're Lucas Quinn." Matty interrupts, suddenly staring hard at the side of Lucas's face from the backseat. It's intense and Lucas feels deeply seen.

"I am, yeah." Lucas grins, catching another glimpse of Matty in the rearview as the light turns green.

"No, you're not. You can't be." Matty crosses their arms over their chest and slumps back against the door with a huff. Lucas is confused for at least the third time this evening.

"I'm not? Pretty sure that's what they've stamped in my passport." Lucas wonders vaguely if Matty is a reader. Likely, since they seem to know his work.

"You can't be Lucas Quinn because I can't be in the back of Lucas Quinn's car on the way to A&E after crawling to Lucas Quinn's door with a broken ankle and potentially bleeding on Lucas Quinn's dog's pillow." Matty takes the little clip out of the front of their hair and starts to fidget and fuss with it.

"You're bleeding?" Lucas focuses on that, since the rest he isn't sure how to address.

"Not currently, but I may implode from embarrassment in which case I suspect that yes, there may be blood." Matty says all this in a very matter of fact way. Lucas is fascinated by their mind, the way they shape their thoughts and share them as if they're anything less than extraordinary.

"So you read." Lucas isn't asking a question. It's clear at this point that Matty knows his books, and potentially even enjoys them.

"Only every moment I'm alive." Matty allows themself a small smile that Lucas catches before it's tucked away again.

"Is that what you do for work, then?" Lucas asks, hoping it isn't overstepping. But they're already talking about Lucas's work so hopefully it's safe enough, and maybe a helpful distraction with a few minutes left in their drive.

"No, I was never any good with words besides reading them, and I don't know of a career that pays me to read and keeps me in Louboutin's." Matty sighs again and stares wistfully at their feet. "Then again, my beloved Louboutin's betrayed me tonight...I'm a photographer. Of sorts."

"Any particular style?" Lucas can so easily picture Matty's tall frame completed by a six inch heel, just as suited to them as when they're out on one of their morning jogs in grungy trainers. If there's one thing Matty has, it's range.

"The Iriza. Gorgeous silhouette and an open arch with a cutout vamp." Matty's voice has this velveteen quality, especially when talking about something they have a passion for. Lucas is already learning so much, and yet he doesn't even know Matty's last name or where they're from.

"Noted. But I was asking about your photography." Lucas smiles as he turns a corner. He has no fucking clue what an Iriza is, but he can google it later. Not far from the hospital now.

"Bit of everything. I don't like to choose, I suppose. One day I'll photograph a wedding and the next I'll work on a print campaign for some new fashion house. I'll work with anyone so long as they pay my rates and aren't a bellend." Matty makes it sound so simple, but Lucas knows how much housing costs where they live and Matty must be doing well in their field to afford renting a house in Brighton on their own.

"This may be a wild question, but you mentioned knowing a Zakir earlier and now I know you sometimes work with models. Do you by any chance know Zakir Akhtar?" Lucas is almost positive it's a different Zakir, but it can't hurt to ask.

"And how is it you know my codependent badger?" Matty asks, their left hand landing on Lucas's bicep as they lean forward in their seat, carefully avoiding shifting their ankle from the pillow. They seem genuinely excited to have this personal connection and Lucas is glad he brought it up.

"His partner is my best mate: Nathan Davis." Lucas grins, trying not to crash his very sensible Mini Countryman by recklessly turning around to flirt with his injured passenger. "And with Nathan comes Zakir, so he's also one of my best mates by extension."

"Nathan's such a nerd. But he's good to Zakir so he can stay." Matty adds nonchalantly, as if it was actually up to them.

Lucas snorts, covering his mouth as he continues to laugh. "Pretty sure they're both nerds. That's literally how they met."

"How is it I've never seen them coming round your place? Or that you've never noticed Zakir coming round mine?" Matty asks, hand squeezing Lucas's bicep once more before falling away again. Lucas already misses the warmth.

"We like to go out, have a picnic or see a show, maybe visit a club. I don't leave the house much these days if Nathan doesn't make me." Lucas turns another corner and the hospital entrance is in view. One step closer to getting Matty back on their feet. "And badgers are notoriously good at hiding."

"I suppose I'm similar: home if I'm not working. I wonder if Zakir's even realised that my neighbour Lucas is the same Lucas that helped Nathan plan his surprise birthday party." Matty wonders aloud, and Lucas doesn't miss the clear implications that 1) Matty has clearly mentioned him to Zakir and 2) Matty knows quite a bit about Lucas from Zakir even if neither of them was aware.

And if Lucas knows anything about Zakir, it's that he definitely put two and two together immediately but decided not to meddle. Or, significantly more likely, that Nathan told them not to and Zakir begrudgingly agreed.

"So you know him well, then." Lucas finds a parking space, surprised to see that there doesn't appear to be *that* much of a crowd. Then again, most of the A&E will be full of night out injuries or those who decided to throw a few punches over their team losing a game of football. It's Saturday.

"Three months since we met and it's as if we were separated at badger birth." Matty agrees, sitting up and catching their breath when their ankle moves in response. Lucas wonders how much Matty is holding back because if he were in the same position he'd be significantly less composed. "Could, um, if you don't mind, could you help me inside?"

"I was actually planning to stay. Be here if you need anything and give you a ride home." Lucas shuts the car off and turns around in his seat. It's hard to see Matty from this angle, but he wants to make sure he establishes whatever boundary Matty is comfortable with before they go inside.

"You don't have to do that. I can...figure it out." Matty visibly retreats back into themself, adjusting the skirt of their dress and sighing. "And you'll have to pay for parking."

Lucas slowly reaches out until his hand is hovering over Matty's, carefully laying it on top. "I'm offering. Believe me, I'm not missing anything at home. But I'll leave if you'd rather. Just figured since we're neighbours and all, and the dogs may have me for supper if I left you here to fend for yourself." He hears a small, withheld laugh so he gives Matty's hand a quick squeeze.

"I'd appreciate the company, but on one condition." Matty glances up at Lucas when he removes his hand again, looking so vulnerable and shy it's like the past few minutes of conversation never happened.

Lucas nods and gestures as if to say, *go on then*. Matty pauses, fiddling with their own fingers before pulling their hair away from their face with the clip again, clearly preparing themself. "Don't be a bastard."

"Ah, well unfortunately *that* I cannot promise." Lucas gives Matty a sideways grin when they look up at him in confusion. "See, my parents were never married and then my dad ran off before I made it to my first birthday, so I am technically and definitionally a bastard."

"Lucas..." Matty rolls their eyes and swats at Lucas playfully, a hint of colour at the apples of their cheeks. Lucas wonders if they have any idea how gorgeous they are, even when dealing with their emergency injury. "It's just...doctors are complicated for me. The whole hospital situation and the ignorant questions and how I'm often treated. So if you're going to be a prick, I can't deal with that on top of...everything else."

"Oh, Matty, that's..." Lucas is caught off guard by the sudden sincerity. They haven't even approached the topic of identity for either of them. Sure, they live in Brighton and it's sort of an unofficial queer capitol, but still. Lucas knows how cruel the world can be, and he hates the idea of that cruelty aimed at someone like Matty who seems to have a very gentle soul. "I won't be a bastard. You have my word."

"Please don't promise that if you don't mean it." Matty is staring hard at Lucas, borderline fierce, such a contrast to the coy, quiet side that they've shown thus far. "I'd rather you dump me in the car park and have it over with than let me think I have a friend in there only to find out I was wrong."

"You have me, for what I'm worth, in the car park or the hospital or anywhere at all. We don't have to be mates for me to be a decent lad, alright?" Lucas wishes he didn't understand where this need to protect themself is coming from, but between Lucas's own life, some of his dearest friends, and the people he's gotten to know through his work, he's very familiar with the worst case scenarios that Matty is imagining for themself.

Medical care for queer people is complicated, never knowing when a nurse or a doctor is going to prioritise their bigotry or ignorance over a queer patient's health. Of course, there's many wonderful providers in the NHS, but Lucas has heard stories of people being refused treatment, repeatedly misgendered, or much worse. Matty's concern is unfortunately warranted.

"If Zakir and Nathan keep you around, that means your word is worth something." Matty is still considering, and Lucas is sure that part of the reason Matty has kept their distance since moving in next door is a lack of trust likely due to years of protecting themself to survive. "And I appreciate the help."

Lucas nods, not looking away because he wants Matty to understand how sincere he is. It doesn't matter that he's completely enchanted by Matty, that they have friends in common, that they're neighbours. Someone in his community is asking him for support and Lucas will absolutely be there if and when he's needed. "Now can we get you inside to get that horror show x-rayed?"

"Please. It does hurt quite badly and it's developed a heartbeat. Maybe I should give it a name." Matty waits to move until Lucas is there to help them. Lucas retrieves the slides he mentioned earlier, which aren't ideal, but they fit over Matty's swollen limb. They're certainly better than barefoot.

"Might be a long wait. I'll bring the pillow." Lucas reaches inside for it, Matty holding themself up against the side of Lucas's car and definitely appearing to be in pain. Either the pain is getting worse or Matty is hiding it less. Potentially both. "We can probably get you a wheelchair once we're inside, but lean on me til then, yeah?"

"I'm feeling slightly faint so if I collapse on you don't be alarmed." Matty says when they're halfway to the hospital entrance, out of breath and occasionally holding in a shout when their ankle jostles just a centimetre too far. "It'd be very theatrical of me, wilting away like a wounded flower in your arms."

"Well if you must collapse somewhere, the hospital is the place for it. But let's hope it won't come to that." Lucas has the pillow tucked beneath his free arm, glad he thought to bring it, because the closer they get to the doors the more he realises how busy they are.

Inside the hospital and into the A&E unit takes them a while. Lucas can't imagine how Matty would have accomplished this on their own. He spent a fair bit of time in a hospital setting growing up, with his mum being a nurse and all that came after, so he's more familiar than most with the general concept and expectations for a visit.

Deciding to share a bit of himself with Matty both as a distraction and a sign of mutual trust, Lucas says, "You know, my mum was a nurse midwife. A remarkable person, honestly. Learned so much from her."

"Up north?" Matty asks, and Lucas assumes it's because of his accent. He makes a mental note that Matty is observant as well as the dozen other attributes he's catalogued so far.

"Barnsley. My family is still there. I'm the only rebel who drifted south." Lucas pauses their progress for a moment.

Matty is doing a remarkable job, but their breathing is laboured and they still have some disjointed walking to accomplish.

"Me as well. Family is in a town called Mobberley. Well, my sister Cara's in Manchester now, but that's not far." Matty leans against the nearest wall, their head falling back while they take a few deep breaths. "I swear I'm fit. Run every day."

"I know." Lucas says before he realises how that sounds. When Matty gives him a curious smile and head tilt he qualifies, "It's just...neighbours. I've seen you heading out a few times, or when I'm on walks with the girls around the neighbourhood."

"You like what you saw?" Matty asks, and now that's definitely a smirk that Lucas detects. Matty is so much more than a pretty face and a fit body. Lucas is in a delicious amount of trouble.

"Might have." Lucas winks, reaching for Matty again to get them the rest of the way to A&E reception. Now isn't the best time to flirt. "Maybe we can talk about it over that cuppa you said you'd get back to me about."

"I did say that, yes. But now that Zakir's involved I may need their permission." Matty puts their arm back around Lucas's shoulder and starts hopping again, barely wincing, but Lucas still notices. He wonders why Matty is so competent at shielding their reaction to so much pain, and when Lucas thinks for more than a second it gets very dark and sad and now is decidedly not the moment for that.

"And why is Zakir involved?" Lucas has nothing to worry about if tea is up to Zakir. He adores Lucas, even if they fight

25

like hormonal cats half the time. Once Zakir realised Lucas wasn't a threat to his relationship with Nathan, the three of them have been like family.

"Codependent badgers, or haven't you been listening?" Matty manages to tease, and Lucas truly admires their dedication to a through line. Maybe one day he'll get to hear all the thoughts that Matty carefully pieces together, one syllable at a time, each more interesting than the last.

"Speaking of, do you need me to ring the badger or anyone else?" Lucas asks as they get in the queue for the person responsible for check in. There's two injuries ahead of them: one appears to be an allergic reaction of some kind, the other a mishap with what he assumes was a kitchen gadget.

"He's the one who told me to put on my big girl boots and crawl over to your door for help since I absolutely refused to consider an ambulance." Matty leans even heavier on Lucas but it's not uncomfortable, rather more familiar than anything, like Matty is slowly warming to the idea of trusting Lucas.

"Ambulance didn't go with the outfit?" Lucas guesses, and the laugh he gets pressed into his shoulder in response will be worth at least an essay in one of his books. Maybe even a standalone release.

Matty falls suddenly quiet as they shuffle forward, one less person ahead of them in line. They move their lips closer to Lucas's ear to mutter, "Remember what you promised me."

Lucas only nods, giving Matty's waist a gentle squeeze to acknowledge that he heard them and understood the meaning behind it. Matty keeps quiet, still leaning heavily, so

Lucas follows their lead and just waits. It's not as if there's any way to speed up getting Matty help now that they're here. Lucas knows that since Matty's ankle isn't life threatening they're likely going to be here well past midnight.

"You want me to..." Lucas tilts his head in the direction of a few open seats, wondering if Matty wants some privacy to get checked in. But Matty shakes their head no and widens their eyes slightly, asking Lucas to stay. "Alright."

The check in process goes as Lucas expected. Matty gives their information to the staff member behind the glass, and Lucas learns Matty's full name (Matthew Camden). He's aware it's a privilege, especially when Matty leans their head on his shoulder for the tiniest moment once it's been said. With only a few other questions to complete the registration, Matty winces while showing their ankle and explaining how they tripped and broke it just a few hours earlier.

The other person grimaces in sympathy and types away on the computer, eventually telling them both to take a seat and that someone would be out as soon as they could to assess Matty and get them back to a room to be seen by a provider. Their instructions all but confirm that they may be waiting a while as the A&E is expectedly busy tonight.

"There's a few extra seats there. Could put your leg up on the pillow." Lucas suggests, pointing out a set of three chairs off to their right and waiting for a response.

"Will Annie be alright with me getting hospital germs all over her car pillow?" Matty asks, letting Lucas guide them in the indicated direction.

"How'd you know it was Annie's?" Lucas wonders if it's possible to fall in love in less than an hour. Sure, a hospital isn't an ideal location, and a broken ankle isn't exactly a meet cute, but Matty is...Matty is...Matty. The more Lucas learns and the more Matty shows who they are, Lucas wonders if this whole neighbour situation isn't something like fate.

"Has her vibes. Hallie would never go for something as basic as a dog bone print. She seems more like a polka dot girl. No stripes though." Matty wrinkles their nose and Lucas wants to give it a boop. Maybe kiss away the scrunch and bring back their smile.

"You sure you aren't secretly a dog whisperer?" Lucas asks, helping Matty into the chair and lifting their leg up and onto the pillow in question. No, Annie absolutely will not mind, and it's touching that Matty would think to ask, even if it was mostly a hypothetical concern.

"But where are you going to sit?" Matty asks when they notice that the way Lucas positioned them leaves no spot for himself.

"I'll just stand for a bit. Knowing how this goes, we'll be getting you a wheelchair soon when they assess you before the x-rays, and at some point you'll get a room when they plaster that delicate Bambi ankle of yours." Lucas stands near Matty's lower leg, shielding it in case anyone walks too close and bumps into the pillow, or worse, the ankle itself.

"So you named the girls after the 1998 version then? I suppose the 1961 film was too traditional, or you just didn't like the names Sharon and Susan?" Matty lets their head fall against the hospital wall, seeming both uncomfortable and on edge. A hospital waiting room isn't a fun place for anyone, but if Lucas had to guess, Matty is used to stares and uncomfortable conversations, and potentially worse based on what they said in the car park.

"You're really something, you know that? First person to recognise their names." Lucas chooses to follow Matty's line of conversation, always happy to talk about the dogs. "Watched a lot of twin films with the family since we've got three sets among us. I was the only one without a twin in the house. And when I met those wriggling pups who look almost identical I just sort of decided they needed famous twin names. MaryKate and Ashley would've been too obvious, so I chose *The Parent Trap*. And Hallie and Annie suited them better."

"They're perfect." Matty smiles at Lucas. They look exhausted but unfortunately Lucas knows there won't be any rest for them for quite a while yet. "Sounds like you have a lot of siblings? You don't have to tell me, just...you mentioned three sets of twins."

"There's seven of us." Lucas answers automatically before his chest tightens and he feels his energy dim. He doesn't want to do this right now but he also doesn't want to lie. "Six now. But...anyway, yes. I'm the eldest of seven. My mum was the most incredible parent but even I have no idea how she managed so many of us."

Matty stares unblinking at Lucas for several moments. Lucas wonders if he's just said too much, even though he's barely insinuated more than the fact that he's lost two of his family members. But there's something in their eyes, an empathy and an understanding that Lucas doesn't look away from.

Breaking the quiet (not silence, because it's never silent in a hospital), Matty reaches out a hand palm up and waits for Lucas to take it carefully in his own. Matty's hands are radiantly warm and gentle, just like the rest of them. "*You learn to dance with the limp.*"

Lucas is hit with something like grief, but calmer. Soothing, like a warm breeze off the ocean. He's very familiar with that quote, having read plenty of Anne Lamott's work in his time. "I'm sorry if you've learned the same dance."

Matty nods and intertwines their fingers, giving Lucas a tug until he's standing a step closer. "My dad, a few years ago. He was a good man and an amazing dad."

"My mum and my sister Lissie. Both in the last few years." Lucas sniffles and clears his throat. He can talk about them now, sometimes anyway, but it feels like he doesn't really need to elaborate further for Matty to understand. The two of them keep holding a hand between them, Lucas looking down at where their fingers meet and Matty watching Lucas.

"Camden?" A voice interrupts their moment and Lucas drags himself back into the reality of the hospital waiting area. There's someone in scrubs with a wheelchair glancing around, clearly searching for them.

"Over here." Lucas raises his hand and waits until they see him, nodding and wheeling their direction. "You want me to wait out here or come with you?"

"Oh, you're stuck with me now." Matty gives Lucas a weak smile which Lucas assumes is due to the pain. The ankle has continued to swell despite their best efforts to keep it elevated. "I bond quickly."

Lucas just smiles back before letting their hand drop, stepping out of the way so the hospital staff can get Matty settled in the wheelchair. He takes back Annie's pillow, tucking it under his arm once again and follows along as Matty is brought behind the doors and into a triage room.

"A nurse will be by in a few minutes to take a look at that ankle." The medically relevant stranger gives Matty and Lucas both an apologetic smile before rushing away again, closing the door and leaving the two of them actually alone for the first time since their arrival.

Given this is really just the start of their evening, Lucas realises that the girls will need to be let out long before he makes it home. Thank god for Daniel Doherty, who never answers texts but will always pick up his phone.

"You mind if I make a quick phone call?" Lucas asks, waiting for Matty to shrug and start trying different names on their swollen ankle until they find one that sounds right. Lucas bites down a fond smile and turns to the side.

Daniel picks up on the second ring, thankfully. "Danny! Mate, you at home?"

"Course. It's too early to be out." Daniel's bright, Irish voice gets Matty's attention from a few feet away. They perk up and stare hard at Lucas. Again.

"Could you let the girls out for me? Won't be home for a while." Lucas tilts his head at Matty's reaction and returns their stare. "They've been fed, just need a wee."

31

"Awwww, I'd love to see the twins. You mind if I stay for a bit of cuddle time while you're out?" Daniel's dog died earlier this year, and Lucas has offered on more than one occasion for Danny to borrow his dogs to help cushion the grief. "I'll just watch an episode of *Bake Off* with them or something."

"Stay as long as you like. And Danny?" Lucas waits for a questioning hum, already hearing Daniel standing up to walk the few doors down to Lucas's house. "Thanks. Brunch on Thursday?"

"Mimosas, hold the champagne, add vodka?" Daniel's laugh is infectious and clear, even to Matty across the room who grins at the sound. Lucas laughs along, his eyes twinkling as he remembers the last brunch they had.

He's pretty sure that he hadn't planned for that noughts and crosses tattoo on his thigh when he woke up that morning, and yet...Daniel Doherty and all the life that he brings.

"Text you when I'm home." Lucas shakes his head with a chuckle before hanging up and tucking his phone back into his joggers.

Daniel's a good friend and Lucas should really see him more than once a week or so. Get out of the house more often, like Nathan is always telling him. But he finally has the domestic life he's always dreamed of, so something has to be truly incredible to convince him to give up his peace for even a few hours.

"You have a nice laugh." Matty comments, still watching Lucas intently. The wheelchair seems to be alleviating some of the strain on their ankle. "And your eyes get all...happy."

"Cheers." Lucas takes the only seat that isn't for examination and glances at Matty beside him. Matty is distractingly pretty, with relaxed brown curls falling from their little hair clip and soulful green eyes. Lucas reaches out and traces his pointer finger along Matty's cheek to tuck a curl behind their ear, then retracts his hand with a fond sigh. "Sorry."

"Don't be." Matty seems much more relaxed in here than they did out in the open waiting room. Maybe it's the privacy or the knowledge that there will soon be an actual medical attendant to address: "Priscilla."

"Priscilla?" Lucas asks, already feeling another grin stretching his cheeks. Never a dull moment with Matty, even if they've only really been on speaking terms for a few hours.

"Yes, Lady Priscilla. She's been troublesome, but she behaves well enough when I take care of her." Matty gestures vaguely at their ankle before glancing back at Lucas. "Shame she didn't like the new shoes, but I have to respect her opinion. She certainly knows shoes after 28 years in such close proximity."

"You have a picture of these legendary rejects?" Lucas widens his legs, getting more comfortable in the chair and waiting while Matty retrieves their phone from the front of their dress. Are they wearing some type of bra? Or is there a secret pocket in the front of the dress? Matty might also just be magic, able to hide and then reappear objects at will.

"Aren't they stunning? And to think I was going to waste them on a date with someone who cancelled thirty minutes before we were set to meet because he *just wasn't feeling it*." Matty sighs, showing Lucas a few pictures they'd taken of themselves in the mirror to show off their outfit. Somehow they're even more stunning than when Lucas saw them moments after the ankle shattering disaster. "Zakir told me he was rubbish, but I didn't listen...should've listened."

"Zakir does tend to be right about these things." Lucas agrees, wondering if it'd be overstepping to find out who ditched Matty and send them for a long walk off a short pier. "But I'm sorry he ditched you tonight. He didn't deserve you. Clearly."

"He's the best offer I've had since moving here, even if his name was Bridger and he came with a yacht." Matty stops swiping through pictures of his outfit to show Lucas a picture of his cancelled date instead. "Honestly I could look past the yacht if he cared even an ounce about anything I say. Never once asked me how I was, if you could believe it."

"Not to judge a book by its cover but..." Lucas scoffs at the man on Matty's phone. "I wouldn't touch him with a yardstick. He's got conservative twat written all over his massive forehead."

"Lucas!" Matty giggles, but it starts with a squawk, one of those sounds that shows it's an honest laugh, that Matty truly finds Lucas funny. "You're not wrong. But it's been...lonely. Not that I had a load of options back home, I just thought...Brighton."

Lucas reaches out a hand and takes Matty's left in his right, holding it on the arm rest between them with Matty's fingers against his palm. "I know what you mean. Part of the reason I moved here was to feel...I don't know. More a part of the community, I suppose. And it's lovely, but it's still...lonely."

Matty sniffles, the sound making Lucas look up immediately in concern. There's already a tear making its way down their cheek. Lucas tuts and uses his thumb to wipe it away, letting go of Matty's hand again to go in search of a kleenex. There must be some in this room, between the crying and the snotty kids and whatever else that comes through the A&E.

"I'm sorry, I don't usually cry like this. I'm just so tired and everything hurts and you're being so nice to me and you don't even know me." Matty continues sniffling while many more tears follow those first few, landing on their beautiful exposed collarbones before staining the neckline of their dress. It's the most tragically gorgeous sight Lucas has ever witnessed. He would already feel protective of Matty due to his own nature, but seeing them worn down and in pain heightens that need to protect tenfold.

"Here." Lucas finally locates a box of kleenex, walking back over to Matty and holding it out as he retakes his seat. He watches Matty for a moment and lets them calm their crying before he replies to their weepy remarks.

He'd offer to find a glass of water, but in case surgery is needed he doesn't want to cause issues. Sliding an arm around their shoulders in what he hopes is a comforting gesture, Lucas offers what he can. "You have a very broken ankle and a bruised heart and that's quite enough to be dealing with on a Saturday night."

"I'm tough though, like everyone always tells me I'm tough. They talk about how strong I am. Actually makes me upset sometimes because I don't always want to be, right?" Matty takes a break from speaking to blow their nose properly. It's loud and snotty and maybe if Lucas wasn't already half in love he would mind. "I told you I bond quickly, but I don't usually cry on people I've never met."

"Oh, but we have met." Lucas grins, sliding his arm off of Matty's shoulders to let them resettle in their wheelchair. "I see you every morning playing in the garden with the dogs. I notice how you tend to your flowers, moving the pot around to make sure it gets enough sun. You always scurry away from me, except that one afternoon I caught up to you. You're very shy but you change completely with the dogs, like they speak your secret language and know just what to say. You and I may be new to this whole conversation concept, but I know enough to be getting on with. You *are* tough, but you don't always have to be. Like I said, quite enough for a Saturday night."

"I'm so tired." Matty repeats, wiping at their eyes with another kleenex, their nose and cheeks now a vibrant pink from the crying, but their makeup is still crisp. "I'm used to late nights and odd schedules but I haven't been able to find a routine since I moved here. Without one I get moody and overwhelmed and I just feel weightless in the worst way. But every morning the girls are outside waiting for me in the garden and it's the highlight of my day. They're there, with a ball or a rope toy and all they want is to say hello and to share their smiles. And I never had to ask, they just found me outside one morning and welcomed me home."

Lucas worries he may start crying too, because that was the sweetest, most lovely thing anyone could say about his dogs. As they're like children to him, it makes him very proud.

But he also hears the heartbreak in Matty's voice, the loneliness and that feeling of being lost while standing on your own doorstep that Matty is describing. He knows that feeling. "You need to be patient with yourself, Matty. Give yourself a bit of grace. You've only been here a few months and you've been working almost every day. I'm glad Hallie and Annie welcomed you, because you are very welcome here. But feeling settled takes time. My first year here was spent in limbo. You'll find your way."

"It wasn't a mistake to move here. I know it wasn't. But some days I wonder if it would've been easier to stay where I was and just...deal. Grow old somewhere familiar and have a quiet life." Matty sighs, and Lucas wishes they could rest their head on his shoulder right about now.

"One day Brighton will be familiar, and you can grow old and have a quiet life here if that's what you want." Lucas sets the pillow across Matty's lap so they have something to hold then wipes away the remaining tears on the cheek nearest to him. "But first we have to get this ankle healed and put you to bed. You need to rest and recoup before worrying about growing old."

"Can't believe I broke my ankle." Matty puts their palms over their eyes and groans in frustration. "I won't be able to walk on it for weeks."

"Well, you have a neighbour with some free time and the ability to help. And a Zakir shaped badger." Lucas grins, tickling carefully at Matty's side until they give him a grudging smile, eyelashes still damp. "I work from home and I make my own schedule. Just started writing a new book so I don't even have to go to London very often."

"And I have Daniel. Once he knows I'm broken he'll probably show up with a vat of soup and enough pillows to elevate my foot to the ceiling." Matty laughs softly, like they're still deciding if they're feeling up for it. Now that the mask of self protection has slipped away, Lucas can see the exhaustion weighing Matty down from every angle.

"You know Daniel?" Lucas asks, and suddenly the way Matty was grinning at hearing his voice on the phone makes a lot more sense. "But you're so shy."

"As if Danny gave me a choice." Matty smiles, looking down at their fingers as they fidget with the pillow. "He showed up while I was still moving in and invited himself over for dinner that same night. Ordered us takeaway from a neighbourhood spot and helped me set up my kitchen. There's not a force in the world that could stop Daniel Doherty. First friend I made here."

"He was mine, too." Lucas thinks back to his own similar experience, answering his door for the first time to a blinding smile, an Irish accent, and a warm hug. Daniel is the reason he even met Nathan, introducing them because he said he knew a lad that Lucas was destined to be friends with. He even called them platonic soulmates, which Lucas had rolled his eyes at. But here he is, three years later, and Nathan's like the brother he'd been missing growing up. "Always so busy, but he's never too busy for a friend."

"I'm so excited to meet Spencer when he gets here next month. All I hear from Danny is Spencer sent me this and Spencer cooked that and wow would you look at how pretty Spencer is in this lighting." Matty rolls their eyes and takes a moment to tuck their phone back into their dress. "It'll be nice to finally see the person who's a match for Daniel."

"Are they together or something? Thought Spencer was a uni mate." Lucas turns to face Matty with a curious look because how is it possible that they know more about Daniel than he does? Daniel's one of his best mates, and has been for a few years.

"You're joking." Matty laughs and also turns to face Lucas as much as they can given the ankle and the wheelchair and the pain.

"No? I've only spent time with Spencer a few times since I moved here." Lucas shrugs and waits for Matty to elaborate.

"Lucas. They're married. Spencer is Daniel's husband." Matty laughs again, shoving at Lucas's chest playfully. "How did you not notice that Daniel has an entire international husband? You've known him for three years. They split their time between New York, Ireland, and Brighton. Did you think Daniel just went on holiday with him for half the year?"

"Well! Spencer's only around part of the year and Daniel and I usually either chill at my house just the two of us or go out on the town causing chaos. Spencer's never come out with us." Lucas laughs at himself because now that Matty mentions it, those two are definitely married. "Though that explains a few things, like how they always spend the holidays together and Daniel's trip to America every spring. Do they not wear rings? I would've noticed Danny wearing a wedding ring. He's very particular with his jewellery."

"I thought you were observant. You're an *author*, Lu. You're meant to notice these things and write them into your books as observations on the human condition or whatever." Matty grins at Lucas with something resembling a twinkle in their eye. "And they absolutely do wear wedding rings."

"There's no way that I missed wedding rings." Lucas huffs and pulls out his phone again, finding Daniel's instagram profile and realising that most of the posts are Daniel and Spencer together. Maybe he has been a bit oblivious. "Look! Not a ring on either of their ring fingers."

"Lucas. They're gay." Matty says very seriously, as if Lucas is missing something completely obvious. They cross their arms over their chest and furrow their brow, blinking a few times in rapid succession. "You aren't even looking at the correct hand. They have each other's birthstones on their matching bands."

Lucas finds a picture where he can see Daniel's right hand, and sure enough, there's a gold band with a row of peridot on his right middle finger, making Spencer an August baby. "Well, fuck me. They're married. Daniel's got an entire international husband and I didn't notice."

"They've been married almost five years." Matty takes Lucas's phone, quite boldly for someone so shy, and scrolls through Daniel's instagram until finding what they were looking for. "And here's a wedding picture."

"I don't really spend much time on social media, if I'm honest. But, erm...suppose I should've noticed that Danny has a husband." Lucas locks his phone and puts it back in his pocket. "Should probably send flowers or something. I've missed congratulating him on a few anniversaries."

"It's a good thing you're pretty." Matty teases, leaning back in the wheelchair with another sigh. They definitely seem brighter than a few minutes ago, but it's not as if the broken ankle has gotten any better. "Is it normal to wait this long to be examined?"

"Might be, yeah. We'll likely be here a few more hours." Lucas stands up and starts to pace the room. He doesn't do well when he has to sit still and he can't be writing. "You alright? Need anything?"

"Could use a nap and some paracetamol, but otherwise I'm grand. Bit thirsty, I guess." Matty shrugs and brushes a curl away from their eyes. So nonchalant, but Lucas knows by now that if they're even mentioning discomfort, they're in pain.

"Should I - " Before Lucas can finish his question, someone opens the door to the triage room and walks directly over to the computer, not even glancing at either of them before speaking.

"I'm Carrie. I'll be examining your ankle and determining where we bring you next." She still hasn't looked at Matty, and it appears no response is expected while she starts typing. Matty chews nervously at their bottom lip and looks to Lucas, reaching out silently for his hand which he gives gladly. "Once I've completed my assessment you'll be needing an x-ray. Another technician will be along to take care of that."

Matty's eyes are wide and they're still not saying anything. Lucas can't blame them for their reluctance, even if they weren't very shy. This is the person meant to treat Matty's extreme pain and they won't even bother to turn around. It's not about customer service or anything like that, but the patient needs to feel like a person. Lucas's mum always told him how important that was. But either this nurse is having an exceptionally bad night or she couldn't care less about that part of the job.

"Have you had anything to eat or drink in the past four hours?" The nurse asks, still typing away.

"Oh, erm, no. Not since lunch around one." Matty answers, quiet and small. Lucas rubs his thumb along the top of their hand, hoping his presence is offering comfort during this awkward interaction. He knows Matty had plans for a dinner date, so in this case the cancellation may have worked in their favour because they may need surgery depending on what the fracture looks like. "I did have some tea later. About three."

"Any chance that you might be pregnant?" The nurse asks, and Matty makes a noise that could be a hiccough, potentially a squeak. They're clearly surprised and flustered by the question, and Lucas isn't sure what's going on.

"Definitely not, no." Matty looks confused, staring between the nurse and Lucas, and unfortunately Lucas sees them calculating if they're on the receiving end of a nasty joke. It doesn't seem like it, but Lucas understands why Matty might think so, appearing very femme for their cancelled date, still in the dress with the soft ringlets and all their meticulously applied makeup.

The nurse finally does turn around, but to look at Lucas instead of Matty. She gives Lucas a thorough scan and lifts her eyebrows, finally shifting her focus to Matty in disbelief. "Are you sure?"

And while Lucas appreciates the confidence in his ability to pull Matty, this is decidedly not about him.

"Very sure, yes..." Matty seems less suspicious now and more on the verge of laughter. Lucas knows that if they laugh he'll lose all semblance of control, and the two of them will have to be excused to compose themselves.

"We'll need a urine sample to confirm. Date of your last menstrual cycle?" The nurse goes back to typing, seemingly satisfied with just the glance.

"Um...never?" Matty stifles a giggle this time, hiding their face against Lucas's shoulder again. Lucas feels their warmth like a sunbeam in spring.

The nurse pauses her typing for a moment, deciding if that warrants follow up. But apparently not because, "Method of contraception?"

Lucas seriously doubts that she's committing to a bit at this point. Does she potentially have the wrong patient? But she knew about Matty's ankle so...

"Wrong plumbing." Matty answers, and that does Lucas in.

He laughs loudly before pressing a hand to his mouth, watching a proud smile grow across Matty's face. He sees a lot of laughter in his future with Matty in his life. Matty has such wit and humour, a bright daring even in pain.

"Pardon?" The nurse turns back to Matty, and now she's the one who looks confused. Carrie glances back and forth between them while they try to contain themselves because she truly doesn't seem to understand.

"I've got a penis. The whole set, actually." Matty manages to inform her through the giggles. And when she continues to look confused he adds, "I'm a transgender person. So no, I do not have the capacity to be pregnant.

"Matty can have the x-ray safely. No potential foetus." Lucas adds, watching as the fog clears from the nurse's face. To her credit she doesn't seem embarrassed or upset, which is better than many people in a similar scenario. If anything, Carrie seems to realise a more complete picture of the situation.

Instead of making a big deal of it she adds, "Right. Sorry about the misunderstanding. Have to ask, but in your case, we won't need to in the future." And she's back to typing.

Matty squeezes Lucas's hand to get him to look over, giving him a bright smile and waiting for Lucas to return it. Lucas raises his eyebrows and tilts his head towards the nurse to ask *you alright*? To which Matty darts his eyes over before nodding and leaning back in their wheelchair. But they don't let go of Lucas.

"Alright. Let's take a look." The nurse suddenly finishes tapping and darkens the screen, all of Matty's information hidden away again. She walks over and kneels next to Matty's foot, gingerly removing it from the wheelchair rest and starting to prod around.

Matty winces and even cries out once, their hand squeezing Lucas's extra tight with one specific manipulation by the nurse's hand.

"Broken." Carrie confirms, setting the ankle back where it started.

"You're sure?" Matty asks, as if there was any doubt given the bruising and size of the ankle in question. Lady Priscilla, if Lucas's memory from a few minutes ago is correct.

"I'm sure. But we'll x-ray to know how broken and to determine if you'll need surgery." Carrie stands up and re-awakens the computer, typing yet again.

"Surgery?" Matty's voice squeaks, and Lucas slides his arm back around their shoulders. They sound terrified at the thought, and he wonders if they didn't realise that was a definite possibility.

"The x-ray should tell us." Carrie pushes away the keyboard with finality and stops to look at Matty from the doorway, just before leaving. "Unfortunately we'll have to have you back in the waiting area for a while until we've got a space ready for you. Rachel will be back to bring you out again in a moment. Might be another hour or so before the technician will find you for the x-ray."

"Is Matty allowed to have anything to eat or drink?" Lucas asks as the nurse opens the door. He wants Matty to be as comfortable as possible while they go back to the waiting area.

"Should be fine to eat, but something small. And stick to water, no caffeine or anything else." Carrie softens a marginal degree, giving Lucas a weak smile before switching her gaze to Matty. "If you need surgery it would be tomorrow morning at the earliest. And I promise we'll get to you again as soon as we can. We don't want you in pain either."

"Thank you." Matty is back to sounding small, but not upset, so Lucas waits for Carrie to leave before turning to them.

"You ready to be stuck with me for another few hours?" Lucas asks, tapping under their chin with his finger. He's very fond of them already, and they're past the first hurdle of the hospital visit.

"I'm sorry, Lu. I didn't mean for all this to happen." Matty starts fidgeting with their own hands again, eyes downcast towards their ankle, as if they could heal themself through sheer power of will.

"It's alright, love. Let's just worry about getting you back home as soon and as comfortably as we can." Lucas has always been pretty adept at being flexible with his schedule, and it's not as if he had plans this weekend. "Now, how does Lady Priscilla feel about plaster cast colours?"

***

"What's wrong? I mean, besides the obvious." Lucas has been scrolling through his email now that they're back in the waiting room. Matty is fidgety, pulling at their dress and fussing with their hair, itching absentmindedly at their arms and worrying their bottom lip between their teeth. For someone so generally calm it's a noticeable change.

"It's nothing. Just tired." Matty answers, hands back in their hair before scratching at their jaw uncomfortably. Their brow is furrowed and Lucas can see through that answer in a millisecond. It's clearly more than nothing..

Lucas looks around to make sure they aren't likely to be overheard and decides to shift his perspective so Matty feels like their conversation is more private. Sitting back on his heels in front of Matty's wheelchair, Lucas sets a hand on their uninjured knee and waits for their eyes to meet. He doesn't repeat his question, just waits for Matty to let out a heavy breath and mumble something.

"What was that?" Lucas asks, thumb now rubbing soothingly just beside their knee. From his new vantage point he can see the discomfort clear in their posture.

"I'm not a girl right now but I'm still..." Matty frowns, speaking as quietly as they can. Lucas focuses hard to hear them above the sounds of the busy hospital. "I *was* earlier when it was time to get ready for the stupid date, but now...I'm not. But I'm stuck wearing all this. It feels...and when people see me right now they see me in girl mode, but it doesn't match and it's...yeah."

"I see." Lucas doesn't move from where he is, letting Matty have a few seconds to process before he starts in with his response. It's a delicate moment, and he knows how much Matty is trusting him to even bring this up.

"Also my ankle hurts. Bad." Matty glances at Lucas for the first time in several minutes. "And I'm thirsty. My lips are all chapped and the lipstick isn't helping."

"Well...I can help with almost all of that, if you'd like? I don't want to overstep." Lucas is glad to actually be able to offer assistance, especially when they're stuck in limbo just waiting for Matty to get medical attention.

"You aren't. You're perfect." Matty answers quickly, flushing a bit with the look Lucas gives them.

"Will you be alright alone for a few minutes? I need to grab some things from the car." Lucas waits for them to slowly nod before standing up.

On instinct, he kisses the top of their head and brushes a hand along their shoulder before walking back the direction they entered. Hurrying to the car park, Lucas hopes he isn't gone so long that Matty will be wheeled away again to somewhere alone.

Due to who he is as a person, in the back of Lucas's car is his gym bag, containing plenty of comfortable clothes for Matty to change into (they're clean, he changes them after each use). Matty's already borrowing his slides so there's no concern with footwear.

And because of all his younger sisters, Lucas also has an emergency kit of sorts for when he's either back in Barnsley visiting or they come to Brighton to spend a weekend with him and the dogs. There's makeup remover wipes, an unscented face moisturiser, more than one hairbrush, menstrual products, and a few other random bits that they always seem to need at a moment's notice.

Lucas tosses the entire emergency comfort kit in his gym bag and zips it shut. The last thing he grabs before hurrying back inside is the other dog pillow. They're bulky, but Matty may want the comfort.

"Right where I left you." Lucas walks calmly back over to Matty who visibly relaxes when they catch sight of Lucas at the entrance to the A&E. They really do bond quickly, but Lucas isn't objecting. Crouching again, Lucas opens the bag and shows Matty what he's brought, gingerly setting it in their lap so they can look through everything on their own.

"Lucas…" Matty's mouth is slightly open, staring at Lucas with tears held in their eyes. It's not much, but Lucas has been given enough hints that Matty's fairly alone, not used to others outside their family looking out for them (though Lucas suspects that's been changing if they're friends with people like Daniel). It hurts Lucas's heart a little to know such a simple kindness moves them this deeply.

"You think you can get changed without my help? There's a private loo back by the entrance I can wheel you to." Lucas stands up again, propping the second pillow between Matty's right shoulder and the back of the wheelchair where they've been leaning.

"I can manage. But will you, um, wait outside in case I fall or something?" Matty gives Lucas a grateful smile, already less fidgety than before. "I'm clumsy even with two good ankles."

Lucas fake gasps, one hand on his chest. He's very camp when he wants to be. "You don't say!"

Matty rolls their eyes but keeps smiling, zipping the gym bag closed again while Lucas walks around behind them to start pushing, undoing the wheel lock as he goes. Lucas makes a short stop at the receptionist to let them know where they'll be in case Matty's called. It's unlikely, only a half an hour having passed since they saw Carrie, but best to be prepared.

"When you're resettled, there's a bottle of water and a protein bar that I keep in the bag for emergencies. It's not much but - " Lucas gets cut off, one of Matty's hands reaching back to rest on top of his own on the wheelchair handle.

"It's exactly what I need." Matty turns their head as far as they can to watch Lucas for the rest of the jaunt across the waiting area, something like trust relaxing them by the moment.

Matty spends almost ten minutes in the loo getting changed and removing their makeup. Lucas figures it can't be easy in the cramped space, especially factoring in a wheelchair and being hindered by their swollen ankle. He stands in front of the door as promised, in case he's needed, but Matty manages on their own.

The door opens behind his back and Lucas turns to see Matty filling out an adidas tee and matching gym shorts, fresh faced and happy. "Could you help me back in the chair with the pillows? They help. Give me something to hold onto."

"Definitely." Lucas takes Matty in what is now a practised hold, setting them down into the chair. He hooks the gym bag, newly filled with Matty's date night clothes, onto one of the handles to keep it out of the way. "Unfortunately it's back to where we were, but at least you can have something to eat. Did you find the lip balm?"

"I did. You keep a stock of unopened cosmetics for your siblings?" Matty guesses, letting Lucas wheel them across the waiting room yet again. It's becoming too familiar of a journey.

"I always try to have what they need." Lucas confirms, tucking the gym bag back beneath his own chair before remembering the meager sustenance and retrieving it almost immediately. "Here. Water and the protein bar. And if you want to rest your eyes, or even just relax for a minute..."

Lucas holds out the snack and a satin eye mask. Cat and Iris don't mind the drive between Brighton and Barnsley, but Ivy always likes a nap. Hence the eye mask.

"Are you positive you're a real person?" Matty asks, taking what's offered and setting it atop Hallie's pillow in their lap.

"Most days." Lucas chuckles, glad to see Matty take a large bite of the protein bar and hum softly with their eyes closed. He knows well enough the healing power of food after hours of stress.

"Lucas?" Matty finishes the snack while Lucas wastes time on his phone, wanting to give Matty a few moments of peace. "You have something. Just there."

Lucas wipes at his cheek where Matty is pointing, but Matty smirks, shaking their head no.

"Let me." Matty reaches their hand out, surprising Lucas by tugging him forward by his jumper and leaving a sweet kiss on his cheek. Lucas can feel himself flush in response as Matty lets him go again, sitting back in their wheelchair with a sigh. "Time for my beauty sleep."

And with that, Matty adjusts the sleep mask over their eyes, careful to avoid the top knot of curls held back by an extra satin scrunchie from the emergency kit. Lucas just smiles and goes back to his phone, his chest warm with affection.

***

Matty's been sleeping, actually sleeping, beside Lucas for almost an hour. There were even a few quiet snores that Lucas smiled at, readjusting their head when he noticed it slip from on top of Annie's pillow. He's glad they're managing to get some rest in the middle of this chaos, but there haven't been many people showing up after them, which also means that Lucas is optimistic they'll be taking care of Matty soon.

And sure enough.

"Camden?" A new person in scrubs that they haven't seen yet comes out from behind the doors, looking around for them. Lucas waves them over before turning to Matty to wake them up. Better him than a stranger, even if he's newly rid of that title himself.

"Matty, they need you awake, love." Lucas brushes a hand along their upper arm, watching as they slowly wake. Matty groans when they try to stretch their leg and the pain comes back to them. They scrunch their nose and yawn like a baby bunny. Lucas swoons but keeps it internal.

"Doctor time?" Matty mumbles, moving the eye mask away from their face and squinting at Lucas for confirmation.

"I think so, yes." Lucas takes back the sleep mask and tucks it into the gym bag just as the technician reaches their seats.

"Hello Matty, I'm Sarah. I'll be bringing you for your x-ray." In a stark contrast to Carrie, Sarah seems to be all about that human connection, offering a hand for Matty to shake before holding it out to Lucas as well. "And we'll have you head back to Matty's room for when the x-rays are finished. Should only be a few."

"Brilliant." Lucas stands up, gym bag over his shoulder. He leans forward and kisses the side of Matty's head this time, rubbing softly at their upper back to help wake them up, carefully dropping the water bottle into their hand in case they're still thirsty after their nap. "Alright if I take the pillows with me? I'll keep them while you're busy."

"Thanks, Lu." Matty smiles at him as they get wheeled away, waving a little just before they disappear through the door.

It's the third time that Matty's used that nickname, another sign of their growing familiarity with Lucas. He adores the way it sounds when they say that simple syllable: rounded and warm and soft. Like a hug.

Lucas gets Matty's assigned room number from the receptionist who buzzes him back behind the same doors so he can do as directed by Sarah. He's glad that Matty is with someone like her for the x-rays. She seems like just the sort of person that Matty needs right now: no nonsense but kind, confident but gentle. He can relax knowing Matty is in good hands.

Lucas sets the pillows on the bed soon to be occupied by Matty before allowing himself a quick rest in the provided visitor's seat. He doesn't think it'll be long until the x-rays are done, but then will come more waiting while the radiologist reads them and consults with the others to decide on Matty's course of treatment.

Best case scenario, Matty leaves here in a temporary plaster cast with instructions to follow up in a few days for a longer term cast once the swelling recedes. Lucas is sincerely hoping for the best case since just the possibility of surgery noticeably panicked Matty.

It feels as though Lucas has barely closed his eyes when Matty's being wheeled back to him, chatting away with Sarah like they're old friends. So much for the shy neighbour that Lucas has been getting to know slowly over the course of the evening.

"Oh no, were you sleeping?" Matty asks, seeing Lucas stir and muffle a yawn behind his hand. They look genuinely sorry to have disturbed him and Lucas has to laugh a little because of the circumstances.

"Just resting my eyes." Lucas stands up to help Sarah get Matty into the bed. They manage it well, Matty letting the two of them fuss until they're properly settled, one of the dogs' pillows on each side of them while they recline in the hospital bed.

"It'll be another while before we have the results, but Carrie is the nurse assigned to your room. She volunteered to take this part of the unit once she was done with triage. I think you've a growing fanbase." Sarah grins at Matty who waves her off with gratitude as she leaves them alone again.

"You mind if I run to the loo? Should be just a minute." Lucas stares because he really fancies the way Matty fills out his clothes, as if they're meant to be shared. The amount of oversized that Lucas prefers seems to fit Matty well. They look very comfy cosy, just as much themself as when they were all dolled up for their date that never happened.

"Can I borrow your phone? I'll text myself so we have each other's numbers." Matty holds a hand out and waits while Lucas passes it over, pausing to type in the passcode and open up his contacts. He trusts Matty not to snoop or cross a boundary.

"No funny business." Lucas grins, Matty already starting to type away. He's positive that by the time he's returned, Matty's birthday, email, and literally everything else will have been added to his contact list. Is Matty the type to add an emoji to their contact? Lucas is almost positive that they are, so he spends the walk to the loo contemplating which one it'll be.

***

When Lucas gets back, Matty asks to rest again, so he retrieves the silk mask and essentially tucks Matty in, setting one of the pillows in their arms and the other nestled behind their back. Matty smiles with their eyes covered and says thank you, Lucas going back to his seat to wait. He couldn't sleep right now even if he wanted to.

Deciding to see what Matty's saved themself as in his phone, Lucas opens his messages to a surprise. Not only has Matty texted themself Lucas's number, they've had an entire, two sided text conversation. And they've named themself *Broken Bambi (name subject to change) /green heart emoji/ (they/them)*. A phrase with a heart in the middle rather than a name, and it barely manages to encompass a fraction of who they are.

Lucas scrolls through the text conversation over and over again, his smile growing wider with each reread. Matty managed to perfectly guess his responses to their messages despite only a few hours of conversation to go on. Enchanted doesn't begin to cover what Lucas is feeling.

Lucas: *hello this is your saviour*
Matty: *My hero /heart eye emoji/*

Matty: *How could I ever repay you? /blushing emoji/*
Lucas: *fancy a chat over tea?*
Matty: *Alright, but only because I texted Zakir while you ran to your car and they gave their gay blessing /deer emoji/*
Lucas: *still need to set a time and place, love*
Matty: *Tomorrow. My place (or technically Helen's place but I'm borrowing it and paying her for the privilege). 4 'o'clock. And dress smart. Your date appreciates effort.*
Lucas: *how does my date feel about flowers?*
Matty: *They love flowers, but only if you bring your favourites so they have a reminder of you after you've gone /rose emoji/*
Lucas: *i'm just next door you can see me anytime you like*
Matty: *No, that's not how this is going to work, Lu.*
Lucas: *oh no?*
Matty: *No. You have to court me properly. Treat me like a lady or a lord, depending on the day, and I'll treat you like a proper gentleman. But we'll not be rushing into things. We'll have tea and manage the awkward anticipation and flush when we talk to our friends about each other before our second date. I'll not be rushed.*
Lucas: *i get a second date?*
Matty: *You've earned a few. So long as you keep that promise not to be a bastard.*
Lucas: *and how am i doing so far?*
Matty: *I'll tell you over tea, won't I?*
Lucas: *are the girls invited?*
Lucas: *or is it too soon to introduce you to my kids?*
Matty: *I love your girls, but tea is only for the adults. They can come along on our third date. We're having a picnic with Zakir and Nathan (and Bruce, who can run around with Hallie and Annie).*
Lucas: *and has the codependent badger already approved this third date?*
Matty: *He has /two gay couple emojis/ /three dog emojis/*
Lucas: *which date are Daniel and Spencer invited for?*

Lucas: *can't be leaving them out now i've realised Daniel has an entire husband*
Matty: *We'll be having a day at the beach with them for date six, even though it'll be cold. I look dashing in a bikini.*
Lucas: *i'll bet you do /wink emoji/*
Matty: *Put that away. No winking until after tea.*
Lucas: *as you wish*
Matty: */blushing emoji/*

Lucas grins and adds tomorrow's date to his calendar, with a reminder to pick up daffodils anywhere he can find them. It's validating to know he hasn't been the only one feeling more than a platonic connection. And Matty's not in a rush, which is perfect, actually. Lucas wants to take his time, to get to know every inch of Matty's heart, to savour each thought he shares like a new revelation.

He spends the next half an hour deciding what he'll be wearing for tea.

***

"Matty? I'm Dr. Rita Moretti, but you can call me Dr. Rita. I'm here to get that leg taped up and send you home. How does that sound?" The doctor announces her entrance with a soft knock before gliding in like a summer breeze.

Matty's been awake for the last ten minutes, talking with Lucas about their siblings as they pass the time. Matty just has the one, but between Cara and Lucas's many sets of twin siblings, there's a lot of ground to cover.

"That sounds perfect." Matty gives her a smile, relaxed and almost comfortable here in the private room with Lucas watching over them. Lucas is glad the unit calmed down enough that Matty was given a room rather than a cubicle. "Is it, um...how much surgery do I need?"

They blanch slightly at the thought, but the doctor doesn't let them worry for long.

"In excellent news, you won't be needing surgery. It's a nice clean break. If you give me a moment I can actually show you." Dr. Rita walks over to Matty to offer her hand, which they shake with gratitude. No surgery is the best news they've heard in hours. "Looks nasty, but we think the bruising is from you trying to walk around on it after the fall. Should mostly clear up in a few days and then you can get one of those fancy colour casts. Have all your mates sign it."

"Matty, that's wonderful!" Lucas is standing beside them now, on the opposite side of the bed from the doctor. She looks between them fondly, nodding at Lucas in acknowledgement before sitting down next to the computer to pull up Matty's chart. Once she has what she's looking for, Dr. Rita turns the computer monitor to show them the x-ray.

"Here. This is your ankle, and here's the break, as you can see...and here it is from another angle. As long as you take care of it and don't do any further damage, we can get you in a temporary cast tonight and set you up with a referral to an orthopaedist for later this week."

The doctor lets Matty ask a dozen questions about the injury, both medical and just general interest. She answers every single one patiently, giving examples and showing diagrams, and Lucas likes her immensely. She reminds him a lot of his mum and how she was with her patients.

"Right. Let's get you some medication to take the edge off and then I'll call Carrie in here to assist me with the bandaging." Dr. Rita concludes, patting her legs with finality before standing up again and heading out of the room.

"Almost done, love. We'll have you home soon." Lucas reaches for their hand and they meet him halfway, letting their fingers fall together.

"Yeah. Home." Matty leans their head back on the hospital pillow and stares at Lucas with stars in their eyes.

****

"Just a few more steps. That's it." In contrast to earlier in the night, Lucas isn't holding Matty up as they approach the front door. Instead, he watches as they hobble along on crutches, ready to catch them should they stumble on their new mobility aids in the dark.

"These are the *worst*. How long do you think until I can be in a walking boot?" Matty humphs as they reach the top of their front steps, leaning against their front door and waiting for Lucas to join them.

"You'll have to ask the doctor on Wednesday." Lucas leans across from them, also against Matty's front door, face to face. It's the middle of the night and the exhaustion of the past few hours is weighing them both down. "Speaking of, you need a ride? My car's got dog pillows to lean on. Real feature, that is."

"I can't ask you to do that. You've already done all this." Matty gestures vaguely at themself, at their borrowed outfit and their temporary cast and the whole of the evening.

"What's a trip to the doctor on a Wednesday?" Lucas shrugs, arms crossed over his chest. "It'll be nice to get out of the house. Been meaning to drive that way and stop in at that specialty market a few streets away."

"You're lying, but I'll allow it." Matty gives Lucas another grateful smile and glances around until they see their potted chrysanthemums that they so lovingly tend. "One last favour for tonight?"

"Name it." Lucas stands upright, prepared for whatever Matty needs. He's at their disposal.

"Could you dig around in the mums and find my keys?" Matty shifts on their crutches to readjust their weight. It's uncomfortable to be leaning so heavily on their unbroken side.

"And your keys are in the flowers because...?" Lucas asks, already squatting down and shoving a hand beneath the leaves. He finds the keychain with minimal effort, pulling out a shining, almost new key dangling from a plastic frog the size of his thumb. It's adorable and very Matty.

"The dress didn't have pockets and beneath the pot would've crushed my frog. His name is Ben." Matty answers in that straightforward way they have, as if any method besides hiding a key in a potted plant would be absurd. They take the key from Lucas's hand and line it up, struggling for a moment because of their crutches, but they manage.

"I'll see you at four." Lucas confirms once Matty's over the threshold. He hasn't mentioned the series of messages until now, and Matty lights up like a Christmas tree once they realise what he's referring to.

"So you did see my invitation." Matty tosses the crutches inside and onto the floor, leaning against the doorframe instead. It's so reminiscent of earlier in the night that Lucas has a strong sense of deja vu and an overwhelming need to swaddle them in bubble wrap.

"You'll be needing those." Lucas figured Matty would hate the crutches. Maybe the orthopaedist can suggest an alternative until Matty can switch to a walking boot in a few weeks.

"They can wait their turn. I'm busy." Matty leans forward into Lucas's space to whisper, "Don't I get a kiss goodnight?"

Lucas has never wanted to say yes more than this exact moment. But Matty clearly texted that they didn't want to rush anything and it's not that this feels like a test, but Lucas will always respect a boundary as it's been set unless and until told otherwise.

"Hm..." Lucas leans in beside Matty's ear, waiting until he hears their breath catch at the proximity. He'll be replaying that sound on a loop until he sees them tomorrow. "Ask me again after tea."

Lucas kisses their cheek and darts away, hands in his pockets as he hurries down the stairs. "Goodnight, Bambi."

Matty has one hand on their anointed cheek as they wave with the other, body slumped against the doorframe. "Night..."

62

PART THREE

Lucas's Sunday is incredibly normal considering the night that preceded it. He lets the dogs out in the morning and watches as Matty props their leg on a folding chair to be able to play with them. Lucas is glad to see they treat Matty gently without all the usual jumping.

With his morning coffee, Lucas plans out his week, then does a bit of laundry, calls his family, and at noon he heads to the florist. He spends quite a bit of time selecting two bouquets: daffodils to fulfil the request and then a smaller, shorter bouquet of seasonal flora to be placed on the table where it won't interfere with their conversation.

He gets dressed in a smart suit, one usually reserved for book signings and that sort of thing, but opts for a very casual plain black vest as the underlayer. Lucas knows he looks good, but he can only imagine how incredible Matty must look. Plaster cast and all, they're the most gorgeous person Lucas has ever known, and that dimple...he sighs at the thought before heading out of his house for the short walk next door to his date.

Before Lucas can knock, the front door to Matty's house opens wide. Matty looks like a vision, more wonderful and inviting than anything Lucas had imagined. A swirl of affection swoops through Lucas's chest.

Matty's dressed in high waisted flare jeans and a babydoll top, their curls pulled back from their face with another clip, this one shaped like a flower. They're effortlessly sensible and sweet, the flare style accommodating the temporary cast quite nicely.

Hands fidgeting nervously, Matty immediately greets Lucas with, "Good, you're here. Was worried you'd gotten lost."

"I'm five minutes early?" Lucas asks, on the verge of laughter. He's so far gone already, the warmth in his chest radiating out until he feels his cheeks turning pink.

"Right. Sorry, just...nervous." Matty stares at the flowers in Lucas's hands, brow furrowed at the double bouquet.

"May I come in?" Lucas asks, waiting for an invitation. Normally he'd hand over the flowers, but given the crutches occupying Matty's hands it didn't seem the thing.

"I told you to dress smart, not sinful and alluring." Matty scans Lucas, starting at his feet and moving up, faltering for a moment once their eyes reach his chest where Lucas's hair and a hint of a tattoo are just visible above the neckline of his vest. Matty's eyes widen, looking slightly panicked, gaze fixated while they chew nervously on their bottom lip. Lucas takes note.

"Shall I head home and change then?" Lucas is grinning so wide his face hurts. This is already the best date he's ever had.

"Don't you dare!" Matty hobbles gracelessly away from the door to let Lucas in, shutting it quite suddenly (and loudly) behind him with the end of a crutch. "So, erm...thought we could sit at the kitchen table?"

"You look lovely by the way." Lucas adds, holding up the second bouquet to explain Matty's unasked question. "I brought these for the ambience. Daffodils are per your requirement."

"And I can keep them both?" Matty asks, tossing their crutches against the sofa. Lucas is really going to have to work on that. Matty can't be jumping around like a broken frog for several weeks.

"I'll be sad if you don't. They're a gift for you." Lucas picks up the crutches again, careful not to crush any of the blooms in doing so, and hands them back to Matty. "Now, hobble to the kitchen for me and we'll find an extra vase."

"Aren't I meant to be giving you a tour?" Matty does as Lucas asks, propelling themself past the living room and the adjacent stairwell but stopping just inside the entry to the kitchen.

"I was around often enough when Helen still lived here." Lucas offers as an excuse, setting a hand on the small of Matty's back to steady them as they wobble. "Save the tour for the second date? I see you've decorated."

"Fourth date. Second date is the natural history museum. You're taking me next weekend and we're borrowing a wheelchair so I don't have to bring these things." Matty disposes of the crutches yet again, this time on the side of the fridge.

"And if I had plans already?" Lucas asks. He doesn't, and maybe another man would be annoyed by the way Matty's already planned out the first month of their courtship, but Lucas finds it endearing, like Matty really wants this to work.

"You don't. I checked with Nathan and Daniel." Matty leans into Lucas until he gets the hint and holds them like last night to help them over to the small, round kitchen table that Matty's placed nearest the back door. Lucas can only assume it's because this spot gives Matty a perfect view of their shared garden and the ability to see if the dogs are out. "I didn't tell them why I was asking, but if Zakir knows, so does Nathan. And Daniel only asked if the dogs wanted a sitter for the occasion."

"And will flowers be needed for the museum trip?" Lucas pulls out one of the chairs for Matty, noticing that the table has been set with an artful combination of home crocheted decor and delicate porcelain. Matty has taste and style in dazzling combination, managing to make the setting both comfortable and sophisticated.

"I'm not sitting yet. I've prepared some things." Matty points at Lucas's chair instead and waits for him to take it before answering the museum question. They don't seem clear on what to do now that Lucas is here, but they can figure it out together. "There should be two flowers: one for my hair and the other to go in your jacket pocket, like in an old film. Choose any flower you like, so long as we match."

Under Matty's direction, Lucas stands up, finds two vases and fills them from the sink before adding the flowers. And rather than leaving the daffodils out of the way, Matty asks that they both be put on the table, side by side. Lucas retakes his seat with his back to the garden and watches Matty add a ribbon around the neck of the taller vase, tying a bow and adjusting it until satisfied, the task executed with a focus to be admired.

"You're the most interesting person I've ever known, and I mean that as a very sincere compliment." Lucas smiles at Matty where they're leaning with one hand flat on the table to support their weight. He's glad to see that even if they reject the crutches, they aren't putting strain on the broken ankle.

"Oh, that would be the autism." Matty says very matter of fact, not even a hint of a joke to it. Like they've learned to own this part of themself as boldly as any other.

"Hm...not sure that's the case, love. I've never fancied Nathan." Lucas rests his chin in his hand, meeting Matty's solid gaze with serenity.

"Yes, but his autism is very different from mine. And I haven't got the ADHD on top of it, though I also find Nathan very interesting, regardless of if he's neurodivergent. He is Zakir's soulmate, after all." Matty reaches out a fingertip to brush along the top of a daffodil, caressing it like the gift it is. "You fancy me?"

"Very deeply, yes. Had an interest since you moved in, but that day we ran into you and the girls greeted you like an old friend, I was sold. They're the best judges of character, and yours shines like the sun." Lucas carefully removes one of the daffodils and hands it to Matty who for some reason still refuses to sit down. "You?"

"Worse. You were like this perfect example of what I've always hoped for and you were just...waiting for me when I moved in. I'm shy, but you've seen the worst of it." Matty sniffs the flower, closing their eyes to savour the scent. "I was worried I'd scare you off or something. And, um...I don't have a great history with dating. Hence all the rules."

"I don't mind the rules. You set all the boundaries you need. I have boundaries of my own. It's not unusual." Lucas watches as they set the daffodil back with the others before hopping over to where they have a tea tray ready to go. "Could I carry that to the table?"

Matty considers for a moment but eventually nods. Lucas comes up behind them, setting a hand on their waist and letting them lean into him for comfort for just a moment, their bodies pressed together with fragile hope. "I've got gentle hands, love. I won't make a mess."

"Promise?" Matty asks, their head resting against Lucas's shoulder even as they stay facing the countertop. They both know they've abandoned the topic of the tray, but it's as good a metaphor as any.

"You have my word." Lucas waits for Matty to shift away then grasps the handles, picking up the heavy tray and whistling at all the treats piled atop it. "You've prepared quite a spread for us. Real posh afternoon tea, which explains the outfits. Didn't know you were such a chef."

"It's just a few things. Figured I owe you a nice tea after all you've done." Matty shrugs as if it's nothing, following Lucas back to the table and waiting until he's set down the tray.

Once it's been safely delivered and Lucas is back in his seat, Matty takes over host duties again, using dainty gold tongs to distribute the food to their plates. "Orange and lemon scone with cream, egg sandwich, cheese toastie in case you don't fancy egg, and both shortbread and ginger biscuits. Made everything this morning."

"This morning? Did you sleep?" Lucas watches as Matty carefully plates one of everything for each of them before picking up the teapot to continue the ritual.

"A bit. Not sure when I'm going to move past this insomnia, but I did manage a few hours before I woke up again." Matty offers Lucas the milk and sugar, Lucas accepting the porcelain milk pitcher to add a dash to his tea before handing it back. Even the tea set is like something Matty manifested from their own mind: delicate and intricate but invitingly domestic. Did they make it? He wouldn't be surprised.

"Hallie and Annie love a cuddle nap if you ever wanted to borrow them to catch up on your rest." Lucas offers, waiting as Matty finally takes the seat across from him to sip their own tea (a teaspoon of sugar and a significant amount of milk added).

"I do sleep better when I'm not alone. *Not that I'm suggesting* - I mean it's only tea - " Matty takes a small sip, both hands holding the small cup while they stare at Lucas. "Not that I'm opposed to it, you're very cuddleable. I don't want to assume, but...sorry."

"What are you apologising for? This is a date. Future cuddling is implied, if we're both keen on it." Lucas reaches a hand across the table and waits for Matty to take it. They set their tea back on its saucer (because of course Matty has matching porcelain saucers) and tentatively accept Lucas's hand.

"I don't really know how to do the whole dating thing. In the past it's always been like Grindr or Scruff or, um...random people at clubs. I've never had the chance to do...this." Matty watches as Lucas rubs his thumb across the top of their hand. Significantly more quiet and timid, they add, "No one's ever wanted to."

"I want to." Lucas confirms, still holding Matty's hand and ignoring their beautiful mini feast for now. "I very much want to, Matty. You're not someone I want to rush my way through. I want to date and get to know you and see where this could go. You've charmed me already. This is exactly what I want."

"You're gay?" Matty asks, unprompted, and Lucas thought that was very much implied already, but if Matty needs the confirmation...

"Broadly speaking, yes." Lucas answers, taking back his hand to try his tea. It's strong and bold, exactly how he likes it. "You?"

"In every direction." Matty worries at their bottom lip again, fiddling with one of their rings while continuing with what Lucas realises is a string of concerns, likely coming from a place of anxiety, or worse. "I'm genderfluid."

"And I'm a cis man." Lucas offers Matty a soft smile, waiting for them to continue. If Matty needs to work through these technicalities together, he doesn't mind.

"I'm not changing my name. Matthew is a family name and I like how it fits." Matty moves their cutlery around their space until they seem satisfied with its positioning, not looking at Lucas until it's just right. Lucas could sit and listen to Matty and appreciate their existence for hours without interruption.

"I've actually changed mine, when I was real young. Story for another time, but my birth father was a prick, as I've mentioned, so once my stepdad came along, everything but my first name was updated." Lucas clears his throat, moving past those memories because he doesn't want to be thinking about that right now. "It's important to have a name that feels right, and someday I'd like to hear about your namesake if you're up to sharing."

Matty nods, accepting the information about Lucas's parentage with a frown, but they seem to understand Lucas isn't planning to share any more about it at the moment.

"I have a penis." Matty says next, and Lucas holds back a small laugh. Not at Matty's expense, of course, just at their straightforward way of bringing it up.

"Yes, you mentioned that last night." Lucas thinks back to that moment with the first nurse, Carrie, and how what could have been an awful memory was instead something for them to joke about together for the rest of the evening. At one point Matty made a *submissive and breedable* joke and Lucas considers it a miracle that he didn't choke on his interest in hearing so much more about that.

"I'm keeping it." Matty stares at Lucas, and unfortunately Lucas thinks he knows where this particular worry is coming from. Who are the ignorant, transphobic people that Matty's been with? And how did they dare to make Matty feel like they needed to justify their own body?

"Plan to keep mine as well." Lucas takes another drink of tea, watching as Matty incrementally relaxes with each of Lucas's answers.

Trust is earned, and while he thinks Matty does trust him, Lucas knows he needs to reaffirm that trust as they go. Every relationship is a constant compilation of trust and communication, and there's no reason that whatever they're building towards would be any different.

"I'm not always a man. I'm often not, actually." Matty starts running their fingers through their hair, separating the curls and then reassembling in a practised motion.

"You don't have to explain your identity to me, love. But if you want to, I'll listen all afternoon. Not in a rush." Lucas chances a bite of the egg sandwich, delighted to find it perfect in every way.

"But you're gay. And a cis man. And, like…I'm only sometimes a man." Matty explains, and Lucas finally understands the heart of the concern.

"You're right, I'm gay. Quite flaming actually. But I've been with people of many genders: nonbinary people, trans men, an agender person, a handful of cis gay men," Lucas takes another bite, almost finishing the sandwich despite his attempt to take his time. It's remarkably delicious and his access to quality homemade food essentially evaporated after he moved South. "Only people I've never really been attracted to are cisgender women, but I'm open to someday experiencing that attraction if it happens. So if you're worried about that, I assure you that's not a concern. Not with me."

"You don't mind that I'm a woman sometimes? Or like agender, or sometimes a gender I don't even have a word for?" Matty stops fussing with their hair and takes another chance with their tea while waiting for an answer. "I've had people, like, tell me to just *decide* or only want to shag me when I'm a woman, or only as a man. It never works and I just end up…hurt."

"Doesn't bother me one bit. I've said I want to date you, and I meant it. All of you." Lucas has been through this type of conversation with other people, both friends and potential partners. Not that he's ever labelled himself other than gay, but he's definitely more open than many gay men. "I don't want you to worry about hiding or changing any part of who you are to be with me. I won't ask that of you. Focus on being Matty and let me fall in love, alright?"

"You make it sound so simple." Matty nibbles at their scone, managing just the corner bit, their eyes still wide and staring.

"It is to me. I like you and I think you're fit and I'd like to give this a go." Lucas switches to the scone as well, finding it delightfully full of flavour, something he'd expect to pick up from a bougie cafe. "You really are a talented baker, you know that? I can't believe you've just done all this yourself, broken ankle and all. I barely manage soup without a mishap."

Matty flushes at the praise, taking another tentative bite of their scone and chewing in silence while they continue to watch Lucas carefully. Lucas lets them process the conversation, finishing the egg sandwich and moving on to the cheese toastie which is somehow still warm and crisp and wonderfully buttery. If Matty ever decides to give up photography, they have a future in the culinary arts.

"Lu?" Matty sets aside their scone and brushes a few crumbs away from their lips and hands. Lucas hasn't spent enough time appreciating those gorgeous lips, but he'll make up for lost time. And those hands...

"Matty?" Lucas finishes his first cup of tea and settles his own hands on the table, flexing them slightly at the thought of having Matty in his arms properly. He's eager to hold them close and whisper sweet nothings and spoon them while they get a full night of sleep for once.

"Could you..." Matty glances around for a moment before pointing at the folded chair tucked next to the fridge. "To put my ankle on. It's a bit sore."

"Course." Lucas doesn't go straight to the chair though. Instead he walks to the sofa and grabs a cushion, then gathers the chair and helps Matty rest their leg carefully on top of the arrangement. "Better?"

"Almost." Matty pauses, watching Lucas again, gaze flicking between his eyes and lips then landing on his fingertips where they remain on the back of the bonus chair. Using their left hand, they gesture for Lucas to lean down, closer, until they can reach. Lucas slips into Matty's gravity with ease.

It's like living a movie from the inside, the way Matty's fingers start at his cheek before sliding around to the back of his head, pulling him in closer. Lucas watches as their eyes flutter closed moments before his own, and then their lips are connected, Matty's like rose petals or warm chocolate, something soft and indulgent.

The kiss is tender, hesitant, until Lucas presses forward to reciprocate, even bent forward as he is to match their seated height. He's been imagining this for weeks in his daft daydreams about being with Matty: late nights in the kitchen, walks through the park with the dogs, soft kisses throughout their days.

"Yeah. Thought so." Matty mumbles, still holding Lucas close even though they've separated from Lucas's mouth. Their hand is caressing the hair at the back of Lucas's head in a soothing, happy sort of pattern as their eyelids flutter to match their stuttered breath.

"Hm?" Lucas dares to press another kiss to the corner of Matty's lips, feeling their smile break free from the chosen spot. Matty's a dream come to life, a small miracle who loves his dogs and gets along with his friends (even without his knowledge), someone who knows exactly who they are and shares themself generously if given the chance.

"Perfect kisser. Everything I was hoping for and more." Matty answers, surprising Lucas by pressing the same hand to his chest instead and pushing him to stand up rather abruptly. Matty holds out both of their hands, palms up. "Sofa, please, if you don't mind."

"We're in the middle of tea, love." Lucas traces his right fingertips along their cheek before resting it there, Matty's hands falling back to their lap. They're meant to be taking this slow, Lucas doing his best to keep them on a steady course.

"You finished your cuppa. I waited." Matty grins, and there's that dimple again, the one that's going to change Lucas's life. "And I let you try most of the treats."

"Was I lured here under false pretences? Woo me with your pretty smile and fantastic bakes, then snog me on the sofa like you've pulled me at the club?" Lucas decides to take a chance, tossing his leg carefully over Matty's lap and straddling them instead. He's very aware of Matty's broken ankle, holding most of his own weight and giving just enough to Matty.

"Something like that, yes." Matty doesn't wait for Lucas to lean in, instead using both hands to pull him forward and giving him a much deeper, hungrier kiss that involves a lot more of their bodies.

Lucas takes the opportunity to grind himself on top of Matty's lap, to tease them, excite them, but not cross into anything properly indecent. There's time for that later. Matty responds in a way only they could, oscillating between sumptuous moans of submission and using their own strength to take over before giving the control back to Lucas, as if testing what Lucas will allow. Lucas is very glad to be discovering first hand that they're as compatible physically as the past few days have shown them to be in other areas.

"You're very good at this." Matty seems to like to talk through intimate moments, and as Lucas finds every single one of their thoughts enchanting he indulges them, kissing across their cheeks and along their jaw when they take a break to share what they're thinking.

"So are you. Might have to dedicate a portion of my next book to examine the art of a proper snog. I'll need to do quite a bit of research, of course." Lucas grins and leans in for another kiss when Matty groans at the joke. They grab Lucas by the hips and pull him closer, hands sliding around to his ass while Lucas tugs at their hair.

It's just as Lucas is considering taking Matty up on their suggestion of moving to the sofa that his phone rings in his pocket. There's only a handful of people allowed through the *do not disturb* filter, so he presses a finger to Matty's plush lips and drags his phone out, seeing Nathan's name on the screen and hoping it's not an emergency. They've had quite enough of those for one weekend.

"Nathan? What's - " Lucas doesn't even get to finish his question.

"I'm sorry I'm sorry I'm sorry I'm sorry. I'm so sorry. I should've known. But you know what he's like." Nathan's talking very fast, and if Lucas is not mistaken, he's a bit out of breath.

"Nathan, what - " Lucas gets cut off again, Matty listening along from inches away.

"Just remember I'm sorry." Nathan hangs up on him and Lucas stares at the phone for a few seconds, Matty's hands warm on his lower back. A moment later there's a knock at the front door that makes both of them turn and stare at it in further confusion.

"Should I...?" Matty looks to Lucas for an answer, and given the phone call he just received Lucas nods and clambers reluctantly off Matty's lap.

"Suppose so, yeah." Lucas helps them up, holding out their crutches until they take them to hobble towards the door, ignoring the neat, unhurried knocks that are now occurring every three to four seconds.

Matty glances through the glass once they reach the door and drops their forehead to the wood with a thunk before begrudgingly pulling it open. "I should've lied about the time."

"Good to see you too." Zakir leaves a very loud kiss on Matty's cheek before letting themself inside, Matty sighing and looking at Lucas where he's standing near the back of the sofa. They mouth an apology, and even if their romantic moment is ruined, Lucas doesn't mind very much. At least that phone call makes sense now.

"Zakir," Lucas walks over to the still open front door, catching sight of Nathan near the edge of the street in his *about town* jumper, clearly wishing he were anywhere else but here. "Did you need to borrow your badger for something?"

"Nah, I'm just here to check how things are going." Zakir drops himself on the sofa, shoes already left by the door because he knows Matty's rules. "How did the scones turn out? Too dry?"

"Excuse you." Matty crutches over towards Zakir and wobbles before falling directly on top of them, Zakir catching their fall like he was expecting it as the crutches ricochet to the floor. "My scones were not dry."

"Nathan, why are you all the way over there?" Lucas calls over to him, keeping one eye on the pile of badger on the sofa to make sure a certain ankle doesn't receive further damage. Somehow, even though he's never seen the two of them together, it's like this is how he's always known them, tangled up and inseparable.

"Because I have bloody boundaries! Unlike *someone*." Nathan has his arms crossed firmly over his chest while he paces. Lucas just laughs and leaves the door open. He'll probably wander inside eventually, especially if Zakir intends to stay. "This was meant to be a walk around the neighbourhood. For *scenic inspiration*."

"The scones were perfect." Lucas adds to Zakir, glad to see Matty glow in response. "Though our date had barely started before we were interrupted by a meddling visitor."

"Are you going to take care of my precious Matty?" Zakir asks Lucas, holding tight to the precious person in question while Matty rolls their eyes and looks pleasingly squished. At least Zakir's being careful with the ankle.

"I intend to, yes. Are you here to give me some sort of talk, then?" Lucas leans back to see Nathan still pacing, about two yards closer than he was a minute ago, still complaining just loud enough for the rest of them to hear. Progress.

"No. Known you for three years. Wouldn't have set you two up if I didn't think you were worthy." Zakir answers, as if any of what he just said makes sense. As if his arrival was planned.

"In what world did you set us up?" Matty shoves at Zakir until they let him out of the hug, but then they lay on the opposite end of the sofa, both legs in Zakir's lap (cast and all) so their annoyance clearly isn't as strong as they're pretending.

"The ankle was just an excuse. If you hadn't tumbled down the stairs, I would've found another way. But I didn't mean to actually curse you so, like, sorry about that, mate." Zakir flicks the end of their cast and Lucas protests with an immediate, "Oi, not the ankle!"

"You didn't curse me. You don't actually have powers, Zakir." Matty huffs, arms covering their chest, so similar to Nathan who's now only about three steps from the front door, still pacing and fighting with himself to come inside.

"What? You ask for advice to talk to Lucas, I tell you to go fawn over the dogs in your outfit before you leave for your date, even suggested you let Lucas glimpse the guy and get jealous, and then before I hung up I said to break a leg." Zakir waves their arms around the air like they're demonstrating their magical process. "Bam. Broken leg."

"Pretty sure it was the Louboutins that did it." Lucas can't wait for Nathan anymore, reaching through the open door and pulling him inside by his well toned upper arm then shutting it behind him. "But also, why the fuck did you go through all that trouble when you could've, at any point in the last few months, just brought us both along to something or mentioned you were the second half of Sonny and Cher with my new neighbour?"

"Because you never would have agreed to trick Matty into a date, and Matty was too shy to come along if they knew you were invited." Nathan answers for Zakir, still standing barely inside the door. "But the broken ankle wasn't actually planned. I believe there was an eleven step process that's now been modified."

"Oh, so you knew about this, did you?" Lucas smacks Nathan on the chest but he gives him a smile so he knows he isn't actually mad about it. His friends just want him to be happy.

"I refused to interfere, but you know Zakir." Nathan looks over at their partner who is currently deep in a whispered conversation with Matty. The mumbled exchange involves a lot of glancing over in Lucas's direction and giggling.

"You suppose we're getting back to our date anytime soon?" Lucas asks Nathan, marvelling at how quickly their afternoon has changed. What started as a domestic, private get together has turned into some sort of bizarre double date precursor.

"Did I mention I was sorry?" Nathan cringes with guilt, but then he catches sight of Zakir's smile and every molecule of his being softens. The Zakir effect.

"He's mischief incarnate. Not your fault, mate." Lucas nudges Nathan with his elbow, the two of them now watching Matty and Zakir together. He feels warm, settled and happy, like this could be the start of something truly spectacular.

"Is that..." Nathan catches sight of a familiar brunette walking with his head down past Matty's front window and scoffs. "Zakir, tell me you didn't text Daniel, too."

"Course I did." Zakir dodges when Matty tries to tackle him in protest and Nathan visibly gives up, falling into one of Matty's arm chairs with another groan.

"I said I wanted today to be *romantic*, not to invite the entirety of Brighton." Matty whines. They keep trying to roughhouse Zakir in retaliation, seemingly determined to ruin that barely contained ankle.

"Matty, not with the cast!" Lucas moves forward to separate them, Zakir trying to bite him like a feral cat, but Matty tugs on Lucas's hand as if hoping to pull him down into the pile. "Zakir, stop that. Go bite Nathan."

"Not in public." Nathan mumbles, one hand still over his eyes. Lucas has never loved chaos more than whatever is happening in this moment.

"I'll just...make myself another cuppa. That alright?" Lucas extracts himself from the two of them and waits for Matty to acknowledge his question before actually moving away.

"Bring me one too?" Matty literally bats their eyelashes and Lucas is definitely feeling some type of way about that...for another time.

"Gladly." Lucas holds their gaze for a long moment, Matty staring back with the truest smile that Lucas has seen yet.

"Ooo bring me one?" Zakir asks, tugging Matty forward for a cuddle. Matty laughs but goes along, still smiling at Lucas even as they fall into Zakir's chest.

"Get your own." Lucas scoffs, turning away and walking back towards the kitchen. Zakir interrupted their date. He absolutely has not earned tea.

Lucas guesses where the mugs might be kept, finding them on his second try, and takes down two mugs that look slightly less precious and breakable than the tea set still awaiting their return at the kitchen table. Lucas takes his time, puts away the remains of their tea in the tupperware he finds, and lets Matty and Zakir (and Nathan) sprawl in the living room while borrowing a moment for himself. This is not the afternoon he envisioned, but something about their friends being this excited for their first date has him smiling while topping off the kettle.

Just as he's about to leave the kitchen, he sees something out of the corner of his eye that has him grinning even wider and hurrying back to Matty in the other room.

"For you." Lucas leans down to Matty's level over the top of the sofa and waits for them to take the steaming mug with both hands. "Teaspoon of sugar, plenty of milk, right?"

Matty nods, tugging Lucas forward yet again to give him a kiss on the cheek in thanks. He rather likes having Matty pull him into their space like this, hoping it's a habit they'll keep as they navigate whatever journey they've started.

Lucas stays close to whisper conspiratorially, "Are the dogs allowed in the house?"

"Of course." Matty answers, nudging their forehead against Lucas's and making him smile in a way that he's sure Zakir and Nathan have never seen. He's never been this infatuated with a person before, potentially because they seem to have all of the important things in common, which is rare to know before starting something new. Plus, Matty's unbelievably charming and sweet.

"Be right back." Lucas kisses Matty on the forehead, ignoring Zakir's teasing coo from the other side of the sofa. Walking once again into the kitchen, Lucas opens Matty's back door for yet another piece of this bizarre puzzle to join the picture.

"Danny, how is it you never told me you've got a husband?" Lucas shouts, tea in one hand, the other holding the door open while he stands in the gap.

"You've met Spencer about a dozen times, Q." Daniel calls back, hands on his hips while Lucas's dogs continue to chase each other around his legs. They don't need much help to keep themselves entertained. "We live together in three countries. Been married for five years."

"Stop shouting and bring my girls over, would you?" Lucas stands back to hold the door open all the way, waiting for Daniel to do as requested. The dogs win that race, sprinting up to Lucas but slowing down as soon as they're inside.

They're well trained and generally respectful, even if they've never been inside this half of the building before.

"After the first few months, Spence and I put a bet on how long until you figure it out." Daniel pulls Lucas into a hug, the dogs already leaving their dad behind in search of other companions in the next room.

"And who won?" Lucas messes up Daniel's quiff just enough to annoy him. It's one of Lucas's favourite hobbies, to ruffle Daniel's hair and watch as he gay panics, trying to put it back together.

"Neither of us. Obviously Matty told you, so we both lose." Daniel sighs, trying to fix his quiff in the window's reflection. "Didn't factor in a new beau who makes a living being observant. That's on me."

Lucas just smiles, looking down into his mug and thinking about Matty. His head is filled with nothing but lovely thoughts: Matty's giggle, their lips against his own, how they hid their frog accompanied keys in a flower pot on the way to Lucas's front door, the way they call him Lu and it sounds like home. "They're special, Danny. I really like them."

"Told Zakir he was worrying over nothing." Daniel puts a hand on Lucas's shoulder and gives it a squeeze. "Nice suit by the way. Almost up to my standards."

"Can't believe you were conspiring with Zakir. And you thought you could what? Spy through the kitchen window?" Lucas shoves him in the direction of the living room, ready to rejoin the others and check that the twins are behaving themselves.

"Could you blame me? You're a borderline recluse and Matty's more shy than..." Daniel trails off trying to find an apt comparison.

"A badger?" Lucas laughs at Daniel's excited agreement, nodding along with Lucas's joke as if he's brilliant all on his own and not just using Matty's own description of themself. Lucas *is* brilliant, of course, but Matty is spectacular.

"Danny!" Matty is lounging on the sofa with Annie on their chest, Hallie on Zakir's lap just a few feet away on the opposite end.

"Hello, darling. Have a nice tea?" Daniel asks, as if Lucas isn't literally standing beside him as the other tea participant. He gives Matty a kiss on their temple, and Lucas feels his chest tighten at the thought that Matty came to Brighton to build a home, to find their people, and here they are, surrounded by love in all its forms.

"Tea was perfect." Matty looks at Lucas, teeth catching on their bottom lip like they're remembering what was interrupted. Lucas wants to be the one biting that lip, but not with their friends here. Not yet, anyway. According to Matty's schedule there will be plenty of double dates in their future.

"They've already snogged." Zakir announces with a smirk, holding Hallie's face in their hands before kissing her on the forehead. Lucas is starting to feel vaguely superfluous, but not in a bad way. It's nice to see all these people in one room, dogs included.

"You weren't supposed to tell everyone that!" Matty uses their good foot to kick at Zakir, disturbing Hallie who huffs and crawls further up Zakir's body, out of the way.

"What have I said about the kicking?" Lucas reminds Matty, sincerely hoping they make it to Wednesday's orthopaedic appointment in one piece.

"That I'm very cute and I can do whatever I like?" Matty and Annie both look to Lucas with wide, imploring eyes. He's in so much trouble.

"Careful, Q." Nathan is flipping through a coffee table book of photography, and Lucas wonders if there's any chance it's Matty's work. He'll have to find out later. "They bat those eyelashes and it's all over."

"Nathan would know about pretty partners batting their eyelashes, wouldn't he, Hallie? Yes, yes he would! I know, I have perfect eyes. I'm glad you agree." Zakir uses his baby voice to speak directly to Hallie. She just wags and wags and licks their nose until Zakir settles her back on his chest.

"Spencer's the same. Fucking hate Florida, but there I was, Miami in June, slathering myself in sun cream and praying for clouds all because he pouted until I said yes." Daniel takes the other arm chair across from Nathan, leaving Lucas the only one still standing. "He sends his love from Lisbon. Called me just before I walked over to see the dogs."

"Stop using my dogs as an excuse. You're a snooper and a conspirer." Lucas decides the best place to be is next to Matty and his dogs, sitting on the floor with his head near Matty's side. They'll have to get more seating if this is going to become routine, especially when Spencer's in town.

"Yes, but he's also Daniel, so." Matty moves one of their hands from petting Annie to petting Lucas instead, running their fingers through his soft brown hair while Lucas shuts his eyes and leans into it with a smile. He could get used to this. "Did you all want to stay for dinner? You may as well, since you're already here."

"Even though we've ruined your date?" Nathan asks, still sounding marginally guilty. Lucas adores him to his core.

"What if we move over to my place? We can order take away, have a proper Sunday night, watch a movie together." Lucas shifts so he can look up at Matty. They're a perfect host, but they weren't expecting guests, and Lucas does have slightly more room since he factored in regular visits from his siblings when he bought the place.

Everyone agrees, Matty surprised to find that Lucas has already cleaned up most of their tea and saying he didn't have to, which Lucas waves away with a grin. The other three go ahead of them to Lucas's with the dogs while Matty and Lucas finish cleaning Matty's kitchen together.

With Matty on crutches, it would've been a difficult task on their own. As a team, the work goes quickly, Matty confirming for Lucas that they did paint the tea set themself when they went with their sister, Cara, to an art studio for her birthday two years ago.

The two of them get along quite naturally, chat so easily, and Lucas soaks up the shared domesticity. For a first date, it's been lovely. He's glad that it's not technically over quite yet.

"Could we maybe, um...cuddle when we get to your place?" Matty turns themself around after shutting off the tap, all the dishes rinsed. Lucas is drying the last plate while Matty wipes their hands on their apron. Lucas had snuck in for a kiss when he saw them tying the strings around their pretty waist, unable to resist.

"I do appreciate a good cuddle." Lucas sets the plate aside and the tea towel with it, letting his hands fall to Matty's hips instead. "Still taking this slow, of course, but I wouldn't mind having you in my arms while we watch whatever *Marvel* movie Zakir's about to choose."

Matty meets Lucas in a kiss, their arms draped around Lucas's shoulders and it feels exactly right.

"Can't believe this time yesterday I was getting ready for a date with someone else." Matty sets their forehead against Lucas's, staying in his space and leaning back against the counter for support.

"Can't believe I didn't ask you out properly, and sooner." Lucas shakes his head at himself, sliding his hands from Matty's hips to his lower back instead. "You're sort of incredible and I knew that weeks ago. Should've made an effort."

"I think...maybe it happened as we needed it to. I was so nervous around you that just seeing you had me running away before I could do something embarrassing. And that was *before* I knew you were one of my favourite authors." Matty moves their face to kiss along Lucas's jaw and neck, Lucas letting his head fall back to make it easier for them. "I had to literally lose my ability to run away and let you catch up."

"You know what I told the girls? That day we first met and I shouted my name at you as you scurried away?" Lucas kisses Matty on their forehead and runs a hand through their curls.

The clip came out when they sat for tea and Lucas is glad they've left their hair loose so he can appreciate it and the way it frames their face like an angel.

Matty shakes their head no and waits for Lucas's answer with wide, hopeful eyes. Lucas remembers noticing those eyes, that dimple, so much about them that had intrigued him from their first few sentences of interaction.

"I said that you were going to change our lives." Lucas kisses Matty on the lips this time, allowing them both a few indulgent seconds before speaking again. "And with the way the past two days have gone, I think I was right. Feels like a new chapter. An exciting, passionate, domestic chapter that we can work on together. I know we're just starting but...I've got a good feeling."

"Me too." Matty moves Lucas's hands down below their bum until he gets the hint and helps them up onto the counter, fitting into the space between their open legs. "Feels right with you. Safe. And maybe last night was a disaster and my ankle still hurts like you wouldn't believe, but it was like getting proof of concept in a way I couldn't ask for. We work, and you took care of me and looked out for me and made me laugh. Think we skipped a few steps, but I don't mind."

"How much longer can we leave those meddling gays alone in my house?" Lucas asks, sliding his hands beneath the sides of Matty's shirt and revelling in the way they gasp. Their skin is soft like warm bed sheets fresh out of the dryer and Lucas craves the cuddle he's been granted.

"Five minutes. Any longer and Zakir will come looking. He's very protective." Matty pulls Lucas closer, settling in to kiss him in the privacy of their little kitchen where the afternoon began.

"I've noticed." Lucas can work with five minutes. He knows they'll have more time, and there's the promise of sofa spooning once they're back in his own house.

As they kiss and smile and enjoy each other's company in the quiet kitchen, the sun sets through the window. It catches on the daffodils, inspiring Lucas to remove one, just like earlier, but this time to trim the stem and tuck it in place behind Matty's ear. One more kiss then he retrieves Matty's crutches (despite the grumbling he gets in return) and walks with Matty back through their house, down their front steps, up Lucas's, and over the threshold into Lucas's half of the house.

They find their friends and Lucas's dogs all on the living room floor, sprawled out together and arguing over what film to watch. Food's already been ordered (Daniel decided on the thai restaurant around the corner) and Nathan even fed the dogs, knowing it was their scheduled time. Lucas and Matty wander into the group and settle in together, Matty sitting between Lucas's legs while Lucas rests his head on their shoulder.

"I could grow old like this." Matty turns to tell Lucas halfway through the movie (the newest *Spiderman*, of course), keeping their voice low and the conversation private. "I'm not saying...I just think this is nice. You're nice. And I could see it. A lot's changed this weekend, but I feel...settled. Finally."

"You think you might get some sleep tonight? You've a long day tomorrow." Lucas asks, his chest warm at Matty's admission. All of their conversations from last night at the hospital are still fresh in his mind, and he's very glad to know that some of that detached, unsettled feeling has fallen away from Matty's heart.

"Think I'll be asleep in a minute. So comfortable." Matty yawns as if on schedule, leaning back onto Lucas and smiling at the temple kiss they get, Lucas's scruff tickling at their skin.

"Sweet dreams, love." Lucas whispers, mouth still pressed to their warm skin, holding them close. "Thank you for our lovely tea."

Matty nuzzles in closer, head resting on Lucas's chest, the light from the telly casting their face in delicate relief. Lucas doesn't watch the rest of the movie, instead admiring the light and shadow as they paint Matty's peaceful features while they sleep, safe here with Lucas and surrounded by their friends. Lucas is in love with this new chapter already, with the people who will help him write it and fill the pages of his life.

It's early, barely a beginning, but Lucas feels confident that he may have found that missing piece, the person who will fit in with his friends and love his family, the one who will inspire his days and warm his nights. Matty showed up like fate but took their time like destiny, and Lucas isn't a philosopher but he knows people.

Matty is kind and honest and intelligent, a combination of spark and grit, a shy badger and a soaring bird. There's so much more for Lucas to learn about Matty and about himself. Love is transformation and Lucas is ready for the change.

When the movie ends, Matty grumbles at being awoken, so Lucas lays them on the sofa while saying goodnight to their friends and tidying up. Matty is fully asleep when Lucas is done, Hallie and Annie curled up beside them, protective and sweet. But Lucas will *not* let Matty sleep on a sofa, not when they're finally getting some rest.

Lucas shakes them awake once more and offers two options: his guest bed where the dogs will most definitely sleep beside them, or a walk back to their own house and a promise to talk tomorrow.

Matty chooses the guest bed, letting Lucas help them hobble along, the dogs almost tripping them every few steps. Lucas lends Matty a tee shirt while they strip out of most of their outfit, then tucks the three of them in with a kiss to each of their foreheads (and another for Matty on their pouted lips), extra blankets and pillows to keep them comfortable for the first proper rest they've had in months.

Lucas lies alone in his own bed, content and sure, staring at the moon until his thoughts of tomorrow lull him to sleep. He'll quietly wake the dogs, let them out, make Matty breakfast in bed, and send them off with a kiss to start their busy day working on the spring campaign for a local fashion house. It's only a preview, a gathering of momentum, but the rhythm of it pulls Lucas into a deep sleep.

93

Acknowledgements

My writing would not be possible without every reader who has supported my work from the very first word, and especially those who reached out with endless encouragement.
I would not be the writer or person I am today without the online communities who have shaped me, and for that, I will always be grateful.

I also owe quite a debt to the friends who have edited drafts, encouraged ideas, and talked me through the tough decisions related to being an independent author. You all know who you are. I love you.

BT

96

About the Author
Briar Townsend is a writer, a reader, and about a dozen other things. Mostly, they are a human who is doing their best. Briar is unapologetically queer and neurodivergent. They find value in writing the stories they always wished to read and representing identities that often go unacknowledged by the mainstream.

***

Contact: briar.townsend.official@gmail.com

Website: briartownsend.com

Links to social media are available on their website.

www.ingramcontent.com/pod-product-compliance
Lightning Source LLC
Chambersburg PA
CBHW022136310125
21209CB00010B/589